Trust Jennings!

Trust Jennings!

ANTHONY BUCKERIDGE

Collins

LONDON AND GLASGOW

First printed in this new edition 1973

For
FELIX OTTON

© *Anthony Buckeridge 1969*

ISBN 0 00 162151 3
PRINTED AND MADE IN GREAT BRITAIN BY
WM. COLLINS SONS AND CO. LTD.
LONDON AND GLASGOW

Contents

CHAPTER I

The Best of Both Worlds

MR. CARTER usually spent the last period on Friday afternoons in reading and discussing the written work which Form 3 had attempted earlier in the week.

Sometimes the lesson went like a bomb: the discussion grew so lively and the class so spell-bound that the bell for the end of school rang a frustrating curfew on an exciting debate . . . . At other times the bomb dwindled to a damp squib and the argument became so futile that the master wondered why he ever bothered to encourage Form 3 to express their opinions out loud.

To begin with, the lesson on a certain Friday afternoon in October had looked like being a good one. Atkinson's essay on *Caterpillars I have Reared* gave rise to some interesting discussion, and Temple's description of *An Encounter with a Dinosaur* led to a lively argument about life in prehistoric times.

After that things took a turn for the worse . . . . The next book which Mr. Carter picked up from the pile was inscribed:

> J. C. T. Jennings (Chief Astronaut)
> > Lunar Space Station,
> > > Moon,
> > > > Near Earth.

In point of fact, this information was inaccurate for the owner of the book was an inky-fingered third-former whose address was Linbury Court School, Sussex. Flicking through the pages, Mr. Carter soon identified the scholar's latest piece of written work.

It was headed: "*An Expedition into Space*", and below that, underlined in purple ink, was the warning: © *Copyright by J. C. T. Jennings. This piece of writing is copyright and may not be reproduced without written permission of the author. Film, television and radio telescope rights reserved.*

Mr. Carter glanced across the room at the author whose rights were so fully protected. In a desk in the back row sat a boy of eleven with fidgety fingers and a wide-awake look in his big brown eyes. He was badly in need of a haircut, Mr. Carter observed.

"What are all these copyright regulations in aid of, Jennings?" the master inquired.

There was a pause while Jennings swept back his fringe and looked round the classroom to make sure that everybody was listening. Then he said: "Well, sir, I'm just taking precautions in case some shady character gets my essay into his clutches."

"Indeed!"

"Yes, sir. That's the proper thing to do, because if you look in the front of a book, you'll find that the chap who wrote it puts a capital C with a circle round it in front of his name. That proves it's his property and nobody else is allowed to nobble it."

Mr. Carter smiled. "You think there's a danger of your work being stolen by some unscrupulous person?"

"Yes, sir."

"By whom?"

Jennings looked him straight in the eye. "You, sir!"

Form 3 swivelled round and gaped at the back-row desk in puzzled wonder . . . . Old Jennings must need his brains tested! How could anybody in their right mind make such a fantastic accusation against Mr. Carter of all people!

The senior master at Linbury Court was liked and respected by everybody. He was a friendly, middle-aged man with a shrewd understanding of what went on in the minds of the boys in his charge, and could always be relied upon to listen to their troubles with a sympathetic ear . . . Not like *some* masters they could name! Take Mr. Wilkins, for instance! Form 3 would have been only too willing to believe the most outrageous slanders about *him*! But not about Mr. Carter. Mr. Carter was different!

The class turned back to the master's desk to see how the accused was reacting to this monstrous charge of literary piracy.

Far from being offended, Mr. Carter was still smiling broadly. "This is most interesting, Jennings," he observed. "What makes you think I should want to rob you of this smudgy-looking page-and-a-half of written work that you dashed off in the evening prep?"

"Well, sir, perhaps not actually *rob* me of it," the boy conceded, "but you might borrow it without permission. Because last term you stuck a great chunk of Venables' compo about bird-watching in the school mag without asking him, didn't you, sir!"

"Guilty!" Mr. Carter admitted. "But I must point out that it's always considered an honour for a boy to have his work printed in the magazine."

"Yes, and I didn't mind a bit," chimed in Venables, an untidy twelve-year-old with a perpetually untucked shirt and trailing shoe-laces. "Actually, I was dead chuffed about it because it proved mine was the only one worth putting in."

"That's not the point," Jennings insisted. "Nobody's allowed to copy out anything you write without your per, provided you mark it with this special, secret sign I was telling you about." ·

The class became interested. "*Anything* you write?" queried Bromwich. "Even your cake list or your weekly letter home?"

Jennings nodded. "It's the law. I've only just found out about it. And what's more, it doesn't cost you a penny to make it copyright. It's a free service."

Bromwich was delighted. "Well, in that case I'm going to copyright my geography notes in future; *and* my diary, *and* my All-World Eleven football team selections, *and* my—"

Mr. Carter raised a restraining hand. If they went on like this somebody would soon start claiming the copyright of the school timetable.

"First of all we'll have a look at this masterpiece and see whether it's worth bothering about all these legal safeguards." He glanced at the untidy scrawl on the page before him. "H'm! You needn't worry, Jennings. Nobody's going to steal a manuscript that he can't even read."

"Oh, but you *can* read it, sir," the boy protested. "It's just that I got a whisker on my nib, and then it somehow got on to the page and when I tried to wipe it off with my handkerchief—"

"All right, all right, I'll do my best," the master promised. He turned to the rest of the class. "All sit up and sharpen your wits. It's not every day that we're honoured by the presence of a writer whose work is protected by copyright."

Form 3 grinned, sat up and sharpened their wits. The Friday discussion was the most popular lesson of the week; for now they were free to comment and air their opinions on any aspect of the topic under debate.

Darbishire, earnest in manner and deliberate in speech, polished his glasses with his filthy handkerchief and made up his mind to oppose any arguments that Jennings might put forward—whether they were sensible or not. Jennings was his best friend, but, even so, he was not going to let him get away with this *copyright reserved* lark, just because he'd happened to think of it first.

Darbishire frowned, trying to think of some similar gimmick which he could lay claim to. What else did they have in books? . . . Let's see, now! Sometimes there was a dedication. Perhaps he could adopt that as his personal trade mark. How would it be if he dedicated his science prep: *To Mr. Wilkins—but for whose insistence this great work would never have been started, let alone finished!*

He replaced his glasses and sat forward in his desk as Mr. Carter announced the subject of Jennings' composition.

The reaction was immediate. Temple moaned aloud when the title was read out. "Oh, *no*! Not *another* of Jennings' corny old expeditions into space," he complained. "They're always the same. They're always about bug-eyed monsters from Jupiter with bulging foreheads and jumbo-jet brain cells."

"Well, why not!" the author defended himself. "For all we know there may be creatures in outer space with fantastic intelligence. Far brainier than human beings like you and me." He paused and eyed the burly, square-rigged Temple with a look of scorn. "Well, brainier than *you*, anyway."

Mr. Carter ignored the exchange of insults and started to read:

"Professor Robinson, the world-famous scientist, hobbled into his laboratory muttering excitedly to himself under his breath. He was bald-headed, short-sighted and stone deaf with a wooden leg, but he was very famous all the same."

Darbishire put up his hand. He had spotted a serious error.

"Sir, please, sir, if he was stone deaf he wouldn't have heard what he was saying to himself if he was muttering. He ought to have been shouting."

Jennings was annoyed at the interruption. "He didn't need to shout. He'd taught himself lip-reading," he explained.

This didn't satisfy his critic. "Well, in that case he'd have to stand in front of a mirror to find out what he was saying."

Mr. Carter raised despairing eyes to the ceiling. The crass idiocy of the argument warned him that this looked like degenerating into one of his less successful lessons.

"All right, then," Jennings agreed. "I'll write a bit in saying there was a mirror in the laboratory so he could watch himself lip-reading to find out what he was talking about."

"Ah, but ordinary reading comes out the wrong way round in a mirror, so he might see himself talking backwards and—"

"Oh, shut up, Darbi. It's a jolly sight better than your weedy old written work on Country Markets." Jennings turned and beamed at Mr. Carter. "Go on, sir. It gets ever so exciting in a minute."

Fearing that worse was to come, Mr. Carter continued: "As the professor crossed the room, his eye fell upon a sheet of paper on the floor, so he bent down and picked it up."

Darbishire's hand was up again. "Sir, please, sir, that's wrong, isn't it? The way Jennings puts it, it sounds as though he picked his eye up."

This time Jennings had a ready answer. "That's quite right—he did," he agreed. "He had a glass eye, you see, as well as a wooden leg."

There were guffaws of laughter all round the room, but Mr. Carter just groaned quietly and closed the book. Really, he thought, there was no point in reading any more if these futile questions and answers were the best that the class could aspire to. Besides, the guffaws had shattered the attentive atmosphere with which the lesson had started.

To change the mood he rose from his desk and strolled round the classroom in search of a more rewarding topic to discuss.

Pinned to a cupboard door was a notice which said: *Bonfire Night. Contributions to the Form 3 Fireworks Fund must be handed to Martin-Jones (Hon. Sec.) as soon as pocket money is given out.*

Mr. Carter had already heard something of the Form 3 Fireworks Fund. Every year as the fifth of November approached, the boys spent a great deal of their free time in collecting brushwood and branches to build the traditional Guy Fawkes bonfire.

Bonfire night was an event to look forward to; when evening preparation was cancelled and shadowy figures in gumboots and raincoats made their way by torchlight to the open patch of ground at the far end of the playing-fields.

For an hour or more the night sky would be aglow with leaping flames; and after the fire had burned low there would be the barbecue supper of sizzled sausage, charred potato and lukewarm cocoa prepared in the embers. Sometimes portions of the feast dropped into the ashes and had to be rescued with poles and dusted off before being passed as fit for human consumption.

Not that the feasters complained! Licking their lips, they would queue up for second helpings of un-appetising fare that would have sparked off a riot if it had been served for supper in the school dining-hall.

There were fireworks too, of course. Beyond the shimmering haze of the fire, the bang, hiss and sparkle of the explosions delighted the eye and deafened the ear, until the last coloured star and streamer of golden rain died away in the darkness ... November the Fifth was a night to remember!

Mr. Carter turned away from the cupboard and said: "Firework fund, eh! That explains the rumour I've been hearing about this form saving up their pocket-money since the beginning of term."

"That's quite right, sir," Martin-Jones (Hon. Sec.) confirmed. "We're clubbing together instead of just getting our own, and we've got a special selection committee to choose which sorts to buy."

"All the other forms are kicking themselves because they didn't think of it in time," Venables added. "Doing it our way, we shall be able to buy bigger and better rockets than anyone else."

Mr. Carter nodded. He had just thought of a suitable topic for discussion.

"How you choose to spend your money is entirely up to you, of course," he said. "But do we all agree that watching it go up in smoke is the best way of doing it? Especially when boys and girls in other parts of the world haven't enough money for food—let alone fire-works."

The class exchanged glances. They hadn't been

THE BEST OF BOTH WORLDS

expecting this. Still, Mr. Carter had certainly raised a
point, so they had better give the matter some thought.

Atkinson said: "Well, sir, if we actually knew somebody who was starving or something, of *course* we'd give
them the money. But it'd be much easier to make up
our minds if we could actually meet them. Say, for
instance, if we were going out to buy fireworks and saw
somebody who needed the money more than we did."

There was a pause while the more imaginative
members of the form brought their minds to bear on
Atkinson's flight of fancy.

Darbishire pictured himself turning back from the
doorway of the village shop at the sight of a ragged old
man shuffling along on two sticks and clearly in the
last stages of starvation. "Your need is greater than
mine," Darbishire murmured, in imagination, pressing
a coin into the gnarled and withered fingers. "You'll
feel stronger when you've had a packet of crisps to
help you on your way."

Venables, in his mind's eye, saw an old woman
staggering under a heavy bundle of washing and insisted on paying her bus-fare home. Temple met an
emaciated cat and spent all his firework money on
catfood. Bromwich bought boots for barefooted orphans
in a vague, nineteenth-century workhouse, and Martin-
Jones fed piccaninnies with platefuls of steaming soup
in a steaming African jungle.

All round the room good deeds were flashing
through the minds of the benefactors: and this was
followed by a discussion about the virtues of self-
denial *versus* the fun of letting off fireworks.

"You can't have it both ways," Temple summed up
when the argument had run its course. "We've got to
choose. Either we hand over the fund to some good

cause, or we spend it on fireworks as we'd planned. Which are we going to do?"

So far Jennings had taken no part in the discussion. Now he jumped to his feet, his eyes sparkling with inspiration. "I've got it! I've just had a lobsterous idea, copyright reserved," he cried. "We'll do both!"

Temple clicked his teeth in exasperation. "Why don't you listen! I've just told you we can't do both because—"

"We can if we do it my way," Jennings insisted. "First, we spend all our money on fireworks. Then we invite the whole school and everybody in the village to a special mammoth firework display. After that—" Jennings' grin was triumphant. "After that, we go round with a hat and take a collection. If we do it that way we'll end up with fifty times more money than we started with, and we can hand it all over to Mr. Carter for his famine relief scheme."

Form 3 stared at him in admiration. Here was a foolproof way of having one's cake and eating it! They turned expectantly to the master's desk to see what Mr. Carter thought of the idea.

Mr. Carter was a hard-working supporter of an organisation devoted to the welfare of deprived children in all parts of the world. Every term he raised money to help combat the problems of hunger and disease, and provide opportunities for under-privileged boys and girls to develop the use of their minds. This term he was proposing to sell Christmas cards and parcel stickers . . . but that was no reason for turning down a well-intentioned offer.

"Trust Jennings to want the best of both worlds," he said with a smile. "Still, I'm all in favour. It sounds an excellent way of helping young people who don't have all the many advantages enjoyed by Form 3."

The bell rang then for the end of school, and Mr. Carter left the room satisfied that he had given his approval to a straightforward scheme that would certainly do no harm and might well do a great deal of good.

In one sense Mr. Carter was right. On the other hand, he ought to have remembered that with Jennings in charge of the project almost anything might happen before the task was accomplished . . . .

And, in point of fact, quite a lot did happen before the Form 3 Firework Fund made its humble contribution to a wider, and more worthwhile, cause.

CHAPTER 2

Science Fiction in the Goal-mouth

THE FOOTBALL PRACTICE arranged for the following afternoon was a game of exceptional importance for anyone who had ambitions to be chosen for the Linbury Court Second XI.

Mr. Wilkins, who was in charge of junior football, was known to be on the look-out for promising players for a forthcoming match against Bracebridge School. He refused, however, to drop any hints about which boys he had in mind, so all attempts to forecast the team were based upon high hopes and guesswork.

Jennings and Temple, both keen players, were regarded as having a fair chance of being picked: so, too, were Venables and Martin-Jones, if they were on form. But nobody could be certain of his place until the team was announced.

Except Darbishire, of course! It made no difference to *him* whether he was on form or not, for his prowess at games was so pathetic that nobody would have picked him to represent the school at tiddledywinks, let alone football.

This suited Darbishire very well. He enjoyed watching football, but he didn't like playing. And the less likelihood there was of his being picked for the side, the better his chances of being chosen as linesman.

As the boys clattered into the changing room to get ready for the game, Jennings was holding forth about the money-raising effort he had suggested the previous afternoon.

"If we're going to do the job properly, we ought to make a guy and trundle it round the village in a bath-chair or something," he said, tugging off his pullover and hurling it at his peg. "About a week before bonfire night would be best. I reckon we'd rake in quite a decent bit if we did that."

"We shouldn't be allowed to," Atkinson objected. "The Head would never give us per to take a collection in the village street."

"He wouldn't know. We'd just get leave to go to the village in the ordinary way, and smuggle the guy out with us."

"And run slap-bang-wallop into a master outside the village stores!" said Temple.

Jennings was unwilling to abandon what seemed to him a foolproof way of adding to the funds. "Well, even if we *did* there wouldn't be much of a hoo-hah, because we'd be doing it for charity." He grinned as he peeled off his vest. "You can get away with anything if you can prove it's all in a good cause."

Venables said: "Matron would give us some old clothes to dress him up in and we could easily get some straw and stuff for his body."

"Right, then! That's what we'll do," Jennings decided.

There was no time then to plan the project further, for the whistle would be sounding for the start of the game in less than ten minutes' time.

At that moment Darbishire hurried into the changing-room with a book under each arm and two paper-backed editions sticking out of his trouser pockets.

"Hey, Jen, can I borrow this science fiction story of

yours?" he asked, holding up one of the books for the owner's inspection. "You said I could read it after you."

Jennings nodded and pointed to the other volume which his friend had put down. "Okay! I'll swop it for that one you've got there, if it's any good."

"Sorry! This one's a library book. I've got to hand it in after football." To make up for his late arrival, Darbishire hurled off his clothes and scrambled into his football kit with desperate haste. Then he took the two paper-backed books from his day clothes and slid them down inside his socks.

Venables watched with mild curiosity. "Funny place to keep books. Most people put them on a shelf."

"My famous, patent, home-made, hack-proof shin pads," Darbishire explained, smoothing his hands up and down the front of his socks. "I got a real jumbo-jet of a kick on the shins during football yesterday, so I'm going in for armour-plating in future."

"They'll fall out when you run," Venables predicted. "Besides, Old Wilkie doesn't like chaps wearing shin pads."

"He won't see them under my socks. And anyway, he's put me in goal so I shan't be doing much running about, if I'm lucky."

Just then Mr. Wilkins' loud voice and heavy footfall could be heard approaching along the corridor.

"Come along, you boys! Time you were all outside on the pitch," the master boomed as he strode over the threshold. He frowned round the room noting the untidy bundles on the clothes pegs and the odd socks littering the floor. "And make sure you leave everything tidy. There'll be an hour's detention for anybody not hanging his things up properly."

"Oh, sir!" the footballers protested, bustling about and straightening their belongings with bogus gestures of haste.

"And what's more, I shall confiscate anything that's left lying about, so you'd better watch your step."

Mr. Wilkins was a large man of uncertain temper, brisk in manner and brusque in speech. Like Mr. Carter, he was fond of the boys whom he taught, but— unlike his colleague—he found the workings of the growing mind difficult to understand. The things boys did and the things boys said seemed utterly lacking in reason to the adult brain of L. P. Wilkins, Esq.

He turned and marched from the room, followed by the boys who had finished changing and were ready for the game.

Darbishire was about to follow, but Jennings called him back. "Hey, you're not leaving my science fiction book in here with Old Wilkie on the prowl. I don't want it confiscated."

The two hard-backed volumes were lying on the bench where Darbishire had put them. Books were not allowed in the changing-room, and to leave them there during football would be asking for trouble.

"I'll nip up to the common-room with them on my way out," Darbishire said, hiding the volumes under his sweater to escape Mr. Wilkins' eye in the corridor.

The ruse was not entirely successful. Mr. Wilkins was standing by the side door chivvying the players out on to the games field as Jennings and Darbishire hurried along in the wake of their colleagues. Five yards short of the door, Darbishire turned left and scampered up the stairs towards the common-room.

"Darbishire!"

Mr. Wilkins' curt voice stopped the boy on the third

stair up. He turned, clasping his hands across his stomach to stop the books from sliding down.

"Yes, sir?"

"Outside!" Mr. Wilkins ordered. "Sharpish, now!"

"Yes, sir, I know, sir. I'm just going, sir. But first I just wanted to—"

"Well, you can't. It'll have to wait—whatever it is. I'm waiting to start the game."

"Oh, but, sir, it won't take me a minute to—"

"Don't argue with me, boy," Mr. Wilkins said, pointing to the open doorway. "Out, boy, out!"

Keeping a firm hold on the ribbing of his sweater, Darbishire made his way through the side door to the junior football pitch. With the master following behind him, he was obliged to walk with extra care; for he had forgotten to put his garters on and his socks tended to slide down over the shiny covers of his paper-backed shin pads.

He took up his position between the goal-posts, wondering where on earth he could put the books he was still clutching to his stomach. The goal-mouth was a swamp of mud, so he couldn't put them on the ground; and anyway, Mr. Wilkins might see them if he did. Fortunately, he was keeping goal for the stronger of the two sides, so there was a chance that the ball wouldn't be coming in his direction until he had solved his problem.

Mr. Wilkins was about to signal the start of the game when Jennings, playing at centre-half, raced up to him dangling a watch that he had just taken off his wrist.

"Sir, please, sir, will you look after this for me?" the boy asked. "It might get broken if I play in it."

"You should have taken it off before you came out," the referee told him.

"Yes, I know, sir. I always do, usually. Only I forgot because I was in a hurry and—"

"All right, I'll take it." Mr. Wilkins held out his hand for the watch and slipped it into his pocket. Then he blew his whistle: the trial game was under way!

The teams were not evenly matched for Mr. Wilkins was purposely trying out the strongest forwards and half-backs on one side against the best full-backs and goalkeeper on the other. These were his "probables"; the remaining places on both sides being filled by "possibles"—except for the second goalkeeper who was an *im*possible!

Thus it was that for the first twenty minutes of the game the play was confined to one half of the field. Darbishire, remote and lonely in his goal-mouth, had nothing to do but stand and watch the distant figures flitting about at the far end of the pitch. Indeed, judging by the way in which his forward-line was piling on the pressure, it looked as though he might survive the whole game without having to touch the ball.

For some while he amused himself by making patterns in the soggy ground with the studs of his football boots. Then he grew bored. It was crazy being stuck in goal all afternoon, he told himself, when there wasn't a hope of the ball coming anywhere near him. He might just as well be sitting in the library reading a decent book.

There was this science fiction tale, for instance, that Jennings had lent him. He fingered the rectangular bulges under his sweater. He couldn't settle down for a good read, of course, but at least he could flip through the pages to see what the story was about.

He glanced down the field. They were taking

another corner kick. They'd been taking corner kicks ever since the game started and seemed all set to go on doing so until half-time. They were all too busy to worry about what was happening at the other end of the pitch.

Darbishire slipped the borrowed book from its hiding-place and opened the covers . . . *The Space Ace Menace.* It looked exciting. Copyright reserved, too, he noticed, so it ought to be good!

His eyes skimmed the opening paragraphs. Then he turned the page and read on, and very soon he was absorbed in the fantastic world of science fiction, mindless of the fact that he was supoosed to be keeping goal in the Second Eleven team trials.

There was nothing original about the plot of *The Space Ace Menace.* By the end of the second paragraph a mysterious space-ship had been sighted by the twelve-year-old hero while bird-watching in a quiet and remote spot in the heart of the English countryside. Two pages later the vessel touched down on the outskirts of a wood and a little green man was addressing the hero in a strange, metallic tone. *"Greetings, Earthman! We come from a far, distant galaxy. We come in peace. Take me to your leader!"*

Darbishire stopped reading and let his gaze wander beyond the football pitches to the patch of woodland at the far end of the school grounds . . . . Quiet, remote, and in the heart of the countryside! Just the place for a flying saucer to touch down!

It wouldn't happen, of course. It *couldn't*! But supposing it *did*! Supposing the sharp eyes of C. E. J. Darbishire noticed an unusual flying object coming to rest—say—on that little bit of rough ground over there beyond the First Eleven football pitch. Nobody else would notice—they were all too busy taking corner kicks. And supposing a little green man with a bulging forehead came sidling round the corner of the pavilion and approached the lone goalkeeper with his inevitable request: "Take me to your leader!"

What would he do? Darbishire frowned in thought. Who exactly *was* his leader, he wondered? Should he take the little green man to Mr. Wilkins? Or the headmaster? . . . To the Prime Minister, perhaps?— or even to the Queen?

Well, why not! In his mind's eye, Darbishire pictured himself in his best suit driving to Buckingham Palace in a taxi with the little green man peering curiously out of the windows.

"That place we've just come through was called Trafalgar Square," Darbishire was explaining, speaking slowly and clearly so as not to confuse the visitor. "The chap on the top of the column was a sailor called Nelson, but he's dead now." He pointed ahead. "That's the palace where the leader lives. You can tell when she's at home because there's a flag flying on the roof. Mind you, I haven't actually got an appointment, but when she hears how important it is, I'm sure she'll—"

"*Darbishire!*"

Hoarse shouts of alarm and exasperation from farther down the field punctured the goalkeeper's daydream like a pistol shot.

Glancing up, he saw that Martin-Jones, the opposing centre-forward, had broken through and was rushing towards him with the ball at his feet. He had outdistanced the defence pounding along in his wake, and was all set for a well-aimed shot at the goal.

Flustered, Darbishire tottered out into the penalty area to stave off the challenge, but at that moment

Martin-Jones steadied himself and kicked the ball forward with all his strength.

The ball hit Darbishire in the stomach. Caught off balance, he flung his arms in the air and his feet shot from under him. *The Space Ace Menace* flew out of his hand and described a circle round his head, the library book slid down from under his sweater and his flailing legs sent the paper-backed shin pads shooting out of his socks to land in the mud on either side of the penalty spot. The ball trickled into the net: the whistle blew for a goal.

The goalkeeper rose to his feet to face a barrage of hostile abuse from his own side who were dancing with rage at his wilful neglect of duty. Even so, their anger was mild compared with the fury of Mr. Wilkins, who came storming up the field to find out what had been happening. As he reached the penalty area his foot caught one of the paperbacks, splitting the well-worn spine and scattering the pages like autumn leaves.

"What—what—what in the name of thunder is going on here?" the referee spluttered as Darbishire retrieved the ball from the net.

"Nothing, sir. Martin-Jones scored a goal, that's all. I tried to save it, only I couldn't quite get to the ball in time and—"

"Never mind the ball! What are these books doing all over the place?" Mr. Wilkins indicated the abundant supply of reading matter strewn about his feet. "Reading in goal! Never heard of such scandalous behaviour! It looks more like a public library than a soccer pitch."

"Yes, I know, sir. They were just a few odd books that I happened to have up my jersey and—er—in places like that. I wasn't really going to read them, sir. Well, only just a quick glance."

"But what were you doing with them on the football pitch?" Mr. Wilkin fumed. "You must be out of your mind! Civilised people don't play football with books up their jerseys. Look at the state they're in! Plastered with mud, and loose pages blowing about ankle-deep as far as the corner flag. Pick up all this rubbish and then leave the field at once. I'm not considering anyone for a place in the team who can't take the game seriously."

This was an empty threat for Darbishire had no hope of being picked anyway. Realising this, Mr. Wilkins went on: "And you've lost your chance of being linesman, too."

"Oh, sir!" Darbishire's face fell. He didn't much mind being sent indoors, but he had set his heart on going to Bracebridge with the team.

"What else do you expect!" Mr. Wilkin snorted. "What sort of linesman do you think *you'd* make? Given half a chance, you'd be running a bookstall on the touchline instead of watching the game!"

After Darbishire's departure, Mr. Wilkins strengthened the weaker side by exchanging some of the players, and this opened up the game and gave both teams more chance to show what they could do.

For most of the second half Jennings played steadily without distinguishing himself in any way. Then, just before the final whistle blew, he found himself with the ball at his feet leading an attack upon the opponents' goal. Some quick thinking and skilful passing on his part enabled him to get past the defence and edge the ball into the net.

Mr. Wilkins nodded approvingly and said: "Nice

work, Jennings!" This was high praise indeed, and the boy was so elated by his success that at the end of the game he rushed off the field without remembering to claim his watch back from Mr. Wilkins.

This was a pity, as it happened, for Mr. Wilkins also forgot about the watch—until it was too late!

CHAPTER 3

Wrong Foot Foremost

Jennings' hopes of being chosen for the Second Eleven were fulfilled when the teams for the Bracebridge fixture were posted on the notice-board during break on the following Wednesday morning.

Temple, Venables, Bromwich and Martin-Jones were also included: but Darbishire—as expected—had lost his place as linesman, and Atkinson had been appointed in his stead.

"Poor old Darbi! That'll teach him to read in goal! He'll be fed up to his back teeth when we come back and tell him what a decent tea they gave us," Venables remarked in the changing-room as the teams were packing their football kit after lunch. "And we may miss evening prep if we take a long time eating it. No need to hurry if we've got our own private coach standing by."

It was this aspect of the travelling arrangements that appealed so strongly to Venables and his friends. Normally, a school side would travel in masters' cars or make use of the local bus service. But the current fixture involved three teams from each school—the first elevens playing at Linbury, and the second and third at Bracebridge. With upwards of two dozen passengers to accommodate, the headmaster preferred to hire a single-decker bus rather than rely on public transport.

"Old Wilkie and Mr. Hind are in charge of our bus," Jennings informed his colleagues as he tucked his football shirt into his suitcase. "So that means Mr. Carter will be reffing the First Eleven and—"

He broke off with a frown. "Oh, fish-hooks, I've just remembered I left my white sweater in the pav after football yesterday. D'you think I've got time to go and get it?"

"You'll have to! Old Wilkie will shoot off his launching-pad if you go trotting on to the pitch without it," Venables warned him. "And get a move on. The bus will be here in ten minutes."

Jennings slammed down the lid of his suitcase and hustled out of the room on his errand. The pavilion was certain to be locked at that early hour of the afternoon, so he would have to find Mr. Wilkins to borrow the key.

He hurried up the stairs to the masters' sitting-room, hoping to find him enjoying his after-lunch pipe. He would ask him for his watch at the same time, he decided as he reached the landing. He'd asked him three times already since the practice game the previous week, but on each occasion Mr. Wilkins had said he was too busy to go to his room to look for it.

This was perfectly true: at the same time, his excuse concealed the fact that Mr. Wilkins was not at all sure what had become of the article in question. He remembered slipping it into the pocket of the old sports jacket which he wore when refereeing junior football. But when he had gone through the pockets later in the day, Jennings' watch was no longer there.

Mr. Wilkins was not unduly worried at this stage. It was bound to be somewhere in his room, and he intended carrying out a thorough search as soon as he had a moment to spare. Meanwhile, Jennings would have to be patient. There were plenty of clocks scattered about the building if he wanted to know the time.

There was no reply to his knock when Jennings reached Mr. Wilkins' study, so he poked his head round the door to make sure the room was empty. Then he noticed a bunch of keys hanging on the wall by the window. Hopefully, he tiptoed across the room and removed the key-ring from the hook. Sorting through the bunch, he soon found the Yale-type key (easily recognised by a blob of green paint on the shaft) which he had often seen being used to unlock the pavilion.

Surely there would be no harm in borrowing it for a few minutes—especially as he couldn't afford to waste time looking for Mr. Wilkins! He would explain afterwards if any questions were asked, but they probably wouldn't be if the key was back in its bunch before anyone had noticed its absence. So he eased the key off the ring and scuttled out of the room with it, as fast as he could go.

The headmaster, Mr. Pemberton-Oakes, was talking to Mr. Hind by the side door when Jennings arrived downstairs. Though time was precious, he would have to put some outdoor shoes on before walking past them, for the headmaster would be sure to stop him if he attempted to go outside in his house shoes.

Fortunately, the bootlockers were close at hand. Jennings jumped into his gumboots, shuffled politely past the masters, and made his escape through the door.

Outside on the tarmac his team-mates, in caps and coats, and carrying cases, had already assembled for the journey. Temple called out: "Hey, get a move on, Jen! The coach will be here in a sec. Old Wilkie won't wait, you know!"

Jennings stifled a momentary feeling of panic at the prospect of being left behind. They wouldn't *really* go without him, he reminded himself: they couldn't very well play one man short! At top speed he raced across to the pavilion, unlocked the door and retrieved his sweater from a peg in the far corner.

As he slammed the door shut on his way out, he caught sight of the bus coming up the drive towards him on its way to pick up its passengers. He'd set his heart on being first aboard to claim the most coveted seat—the offside corner in the back row.

The only way to lay claim to it now was by jumping the queue, so instead of going back to the playground he raced the approaching bus to the corner of the drive. It slowed almost to walking pace to take the sharp bend, and as it drew level Jennings jumped on the step and slid back the door. Nodding affably to the driver, he made his way to the rear of the vehicle and settled himself in the corner seat. He'd have to get off again to collect his kit, of course, but if only he could reserve his place he would have stolen a march on his friends.

Fifty yards farther on the bus pulled up by the corner of the gymnasium and the passengers came flocking aboard, those in front eager to claim the seats of their choice.

Bromwich, in the lead, was furious to see Jennings occupying the place he had earmarked for himself.

"What's this, then! How did you get here before me?" he demanded in outraged surprise.

Jennings answered his scowl with a smile of triumph. "I've been here for hours. You're a hundred years too late if you want this seat. I've bagged it."

Bromwich was quick to spot the weak link in Jennings' claim. "Ah, but you haven't got your gear. Where's your suitcase? Where's your raincoat? You're not allowed to go in gumboots, anyway."

"I'm just going to get them. I'll leave my sweater here to prove it's my place."

"You can't do that! If you go waltzing off and leave it—" Bromwich broke off and his scowl changed to a grin. "Okay, then, Jennings. You go and fetch your clobber. I'll keep your place for you."

Jennings hesitated. It was clear that if he once vacated his corner seat there would be no hope of reclaiming it when he got back. Frowning, he glanced out of the window and saw Darbishire amongst the knot of well-wishers who had gathered to watch the teams' departure.

Jennings wound down the window and called: "Hey, Darbi, quick! Do me a favour. It's urgent!"

Darbishire detached himself from the group and sauntered to the window. "What's up?"

"Will you go and get my case and things for me? They're all on the bench in the changing-room. I can't go myself or some rotten oik will pinch my seat."

As Darbishire darted away on his errand, Jennings remembered his unorthodox footwear and shouted after him: "And my outdoor shoes. They're in my locker. And get a move on, for Pete's sake. We'll be off in two bats of an eyelid."

He slumped, smiling, in his seat. It was one in the eye for old Bromo, he thought, noting with quiet glee that Bromwich had now lost the other corner seat which Temple had occupied while the wrangling was going on.

By this time all the boys had found places for themselves and the masters in charge of the party had arrived. Mr. Hind, a tall, thin young man who taught art and music, was already aboard checking the passenger list, while Mr. Wilkins was standing by the entrance talking to Mr. Carter who had accompanied him across the playground.

"Time we were going," Mr. Wilkins observed, glancing at his watch. "You'll find the pavilion key in my room. It's hanging up on a key-ring by the window."

"I'll find it," Mr. Carter assured him. "I'll just see you off and then get the equipment out before the visitors arrive."

They remained chatting for a few moments longer, during which time Darbishire arrived panting at the off-side rear window with his friend's belongings.

"Here you are!" he gasped, standing on tiptoe with arms upstretched, while Jennings leaned out of the window and grabbed his suitcase. "And here's the rest of your clobber." He passed up the raincoat with the cap sticking out of the pocket and stooped to pick up the shoes which he had dropped on the ground.

Taking careful aim, he lobbed one of the outdoor shoes through the window and was about to follow it with the second, when Jennings called out: "Hang on while I change, and you can take my gumboots back for me."

There was a pause, and then Jennings' left gumboot came sailing out of the window. Darbishire retrieved it, and was about to lob the remaining outdoor shoe back in exchange when, to his surprise, the bus started off without warning.

Taken unawares, Darbishire threw wide of the target and the shoe glanced off the curved rear panel of the vehicle and dropped to the ground. By the time he had picked it up the bus was twenty yards down the drive.

Jennings, too, was thrown into confusion by the unexpected start. "Sir, sir, stop, sir!" he cried to Mr. Wilkins, who was just subsiding into a front seat. "It's urgent. Darbishire was in the middle of doing me a favour and—"

"Be quiet, Jennings," Mr. Wilkins called sternly down the bus. Knowing nothing of the footwear crisis, he assumed that the boy was creating a disturbance in order to draw attention to himself. "You might at least have the manners to take some notice of the boys who have come to see you off."

As the bus gathered speed, the passengers turned in their seats and waved to their friends through the windows. The spectators waved back, fluttering their handkerchiefs and cheering to encourage the teams on their way.

Darbishire didn't flutter his handkerchief. With one hand he waved a brown lace-up shoe, and with the other a muddy gumboot . . . Just like old Jennings to start off on the wrong foot, he thought!

The coach had passed through Linbury village and was approaching the market town of Dunhambury before Jennings stopped bemoaning his misfortunes.

"Rotten old Darbi! He needs his brains tested, letting me go off like this," he complained to Martin-Jones who was seated beside him. "One shoe and one gumboot! Tut! What's Old Wilkie going to say when he sees my feet!"

Bromwich swung round in his inferior seat and laughed merrily. "Serves you right! That's what comes of hogging the best place for yourself instead of looking after your kit."

"And anyway, you can't blame Darbishire," Martin-Jones pointed out. "If you hadn't messed about lugging your gumboots off, he'd have had masses of time to sling up your other shoe."

"Well, how was I to know the bus was going to start! I didn't even notice Old Wilkie getting on. And even then, he wouldn't stop. It's all old Sir's fault, really."

Still brooding over the injustice of fate, Jennings stared out of the window as the bus entered the outskirts of Dunhambury. The windows were steamy so he reached for his handkerchief to use as a duster: and as his hand sank into his pocket his fingers closed round a flat metal object with a jagged edge.

The key of the pavilion! Jennings gasped in dismay at the realisation of yet another blunder. He hadn't given the key a second thought when once the pavilion door had slammed behind him.

And here it was in his pocket! Back at school they'd be searching the building for it by now, unable to get at the footballs, the corner flags or the benches for very important spectators. And they'd have to find somewhere else for the visiting Bracebridge team to change. Still, it was too late to do anything about it now. The best plan, he decided, was to say nothing and return the key unobtrusively when he got back. After all, Mr. Carter or the Head or someone was sure to have a spare key to the pavilion. They'd manage somehow!

He wiped an arc of the window with his handkerchief and peered out. The bus was crawling up Dunhambury High Street in a line of heavy traffic, and the pace gave him a chance to look at the shop windows as they passed.

It was odd, he reflected, that during the holidays when he was free to gaze into shop windows whenever he wanted to, he would pass them by with hardly a glance: but during term time, when he was tied to boarding-school routine, a busy shopping centre seemed such a novelty that he found himself absorbing details of merchandise that was really of no interest to him at all.

He nudged Martin-Jones and announced: "You can get three pence off at the supermarket all this week. It's a special offer."

"Three pence off *what*?" Martin-Jones demanded.

"I don't know, but it sounds a bargain, whatever it is. Prices slashed, it says. Buy now while stocks last!"

He turned away to admire a display of fireworks and Guy Fawkes masks in a nearby shop window; and when the bus stopped at the traffic lights he nudged his neighbour again and said: "You can get five pounds and upwards for your old piano at that music shop. Not bad, eh!"

Martin-Jones was sceptical. "Five pounds! Even if it's just a tinny old wreck?"

"That's what they say. *In any condition* it says on the notice."

"What's the point of telling me that? I haven't *got* an old piano."

"Neither have I," said Jennings. "I was just wishing I had, that's all."

Mr. Hind and Mr. Wilkins were the first to alight when the bus reached its destination ten minutes later. They shook hands with Mr. Parkinson, the games master, who had come out with a group of Brace-bridge supporters to greet the visitors, and they all stood watching as the Linbury teams came streaming out of the vehicle.

The last to appear was the passenger from the off-side rear corner seat. He emerged wearing a self-conscious smile, directing his gaze at the horizon in the hope of diverting attention from his feet.

The ruse deceived nobody. Mr. Parkinson, a portly, genial man with thinning, sandy hair and a generous moustache, glanced at the visitor's ankles and said: "Well, well! One brown shoe and one black gumboot. Obviously a new trend in school uniform!" His smile seemed to suggest that none of his own boys would ever let him down by cutting such a ridiculous figure in public.

The Linbury masters winced with embarrassment. On their home ground they might have been more tolerant of the new fashion, but here at Bracebridge such an exhibition was unforgivable. Trust Jennings to choose the worst possible time and place to make himself a laughing-stock! And why hadn't somebody noticed that the boy was so badly in need of a haircut, Mr. Wilkins thought angrily? His appearance was a disgrace to the school!

The master glared at the long-haired, oddly-shod footballer while, at the same time, his lips parted in an indulgent smile for the benefit of Mr. Parkinson and the Bracebridge spectators.

"Tut-tut-tut! You really are a silly little boy, Jennings," he said through the mask of his indulgent smile. "Surely you can be trusted to look after your own footwear."

"Yes, I know, sir. Only you see, the bus started while I was in the middle of changing and—"

"All right, all right!" At the moment, the less said the better, Mr. Wilkins decided. There would be plenty of time to speak his mind later.

Just wait till they got back to Linbury, he thought to himself! Just let young master Jennings wait till they got back!

CHAPTER 4

Drainage Problem

THE LINBURY TEAMS were escorted to their changing-room in the sports hall—a modern block a short distance away from the main building, where the "home" teams were getting ready for the fray.

On one side of the changing-room a door led to the gymnasium; on the other, to a corridor adjoining the indoor swimming bath.

A feature of the Bracebridge pool was its excellent water-heating system which ensured that swimming could be enjoyed not only in the summer (as at Linbury) but well into the autumn term. Indeed, it was only the expense of heating the water which prevented the bath from being used throughout the whole school year. The changing-room was light and spacious and equipped with showers and knee-baths. Such up-to-date facilities were in sharp contrast to the paint-scratched woodwork and rough wooden benches in the dingy basement changing-rooms at Linbury Court.

The two "home" sides were out on the pitches kicking footballs about when the visitors came out from changing, and the matches started without delay.

The games produced no surprises, no sensational exhibitions of outstanding play. All four teams played well—the third elevens making up in enthusiasm what they lacked in skill. At the final whistle, the Linbury Second Eleven were one goal down with a score of 3–2 against them, while the Third Eleven managed to hold their opponents to a goal-less draw. But though the play was uneventful, an unexpected sequel provided a climax to the afternoon's activities.

As soon as they were back in the changing-room, the Linbury boys made a dash for the shower baths.

"I'm going to have a jolly good old soak," Temple announced, peeling off his shirt. "This is a better set-up than we get at *our* old dump."

The first six boys to be ready stepped under the showers, turned on the taps—and then jumped back gasping as a cascade of cold water showered down on them.

"Give it a chance! It'll come hot in a sec," said Bromwich. He put out a hand into the icy spray and turned the hot tap full on. "It always takes a bit of time to come through."

They waited shivering, with icy globules coursing down their chests, but when more than a minute had passed the water was as cold as ever. "It isn't even coming tepid. It's just as freezing as when we started," Venables complained.

Jennings, who had taken off his boots and socks, but was otherwise still in his football kit, sauntered up to see what the fuss was about.

"They've forgotten to turn the heat on," he said. "I'll go and find someone to fix it." Barefooted, he pattered out into the corridor and made his way to the front entrance of the building.

There was no one about. The Bracebridge teams were changing in the main block, the rest of the school had retired indoors, and Mr. Wilkins and Mr. Hind were being entertained in the headmaster's drawing-room.

Jennings' glance swept round the empty forecourt.

He was not inclined to go farther afield in his bare feet, so he turned back along the corridor to report the failure of his mission.

There were several doors leading off on each side of him, and the first one that he opened led not to the changing-room as he had supposed, but into a small, windowless room in which a light switched on automatically as the door was opened. Along the length of one wall was a panel of taps, stopcocks, valves and gauges connected to a maze of pipes leading off in various directions and disappearing through holes in the floor.

Jennings frowned at the stop-cocks and the criss-crossing pipes. This, clearly, was the nerve-centre of the plumbing system controlling the hot water of the shower-baths next door. One of these taps must regulate the temperature of the water . . . yes, but which? With no clues to guide him, he might as well choose one at random and hope for the best. Even if it wasn't the right one, there'd be no harm done because it couldn't make the water any colder than it was already!

There was a green-painted wheel-valve at one end of the panel which looked as though it might have something to do with regulating the hot water. It was turned to its "off" position, but one good twist in an anti-clockwise direction sent the wheel spinning round to open the valve. Had it done the trick? Jennings hurried out into the corridor and in through the changing-room door to find out the result of his experiment.

The rest of the Linbury boys had given up all hope of a warm shower by this time, and most of them were dressed and waiting to be escorted across to the dining-hall.

"Hey, get a move on, Jen!" said Martin-Jones. "You'd better get dressed right away if you want any tea. You haven't got time to wash."

"All right. Don't panic! I was having a bash at the plumbing," Jennings explained, crossing to the showers and turning on the hot tap. "It should be all right now."

But it wasn't! Although he left the water running all the time he was dressing, the temperature remained depressingly frigid.

Two Bracebridge boys arrived to take the visiting teams to the main building as Jennings—the last to be ready—struggled into his pullover.

"I've brought these for you," said the taller Bracebridge boy, waving a pair of house shoes round his head like tomahawks. "Pinky Parkinson said you'd better borrow them because gumboots aren't allowed in the dining-hall—not even *one* gumboot."

Jennings took the house shoes and put them on. They were several sizes too large for him and the only way he could prevent them from dropping off was by curling up his toes. As he followed his team out of the changing-room, his flopping heels clicked and clacked on the tiled floor like a Spanish dancer performing a fandango.

Tea was a large, satisfying meal of sausage and mashed potato, and when it was over the Linbury teams went out in the evening dusk and climbed aboard their coach for the return journey.

Jennings was unable to follow until he had returned his borrowed footwear, so he hung about in the front hall until the boy who had lent him the outsized house shoes arrived to claim his property.

"Wow! Just look at the state I'm in," Jennings

remarked to his host as the light from the hall chandelier fell upon his mud-plastered knees. "I didn't have time to get cleaned up after the game because I was trying to make your showers come hot, but it wasn't any good."

The Bracebridge boy was a tall, beaky-nosed thirteen-year-old with large ears as well as large feet. During tea he had answered to the nickname of Fliplugs.

"How do you mean—you tried to make it come hot?" he queried. "What did you do?"

"Well, I found a little room down the corridor with a lot of taps and things. I thought one of them might be the hot water, so I turned it on—only it wasn't."

"Oh, I see. Actually, that room's out of bounds, but I suppose it doesn't matter as you're only a visitor." Fliplugs was about to let the matter drop when a thought occurred to him and he added: "I say, it wasn't that wheel-thing at the end of the row, was it? You didn't touch that, by any chance?"

"Yes, that's right. The green one. It was screwed shut and I opened it, but it didn't make the water any hotter."

Fliplugs' jaw dropped slightly and he stared at his guest in dismay. "You opened it! The *green* one! Wow! Do you know what you've done?"

Jennings shook his head.

"That's the stop-cock that empties the swimming bath. If it's been pouring away all the time we were having tea, it must be jolly nearly empty by now."

A spasm of alarm flashed across Jennings' face. "Oh, my goodness! Are you sure?" he said with a gulp. "I never meant anything like that to happen—honestly! I was just trying to make it come hot."

"Not so hot as you'll catch it when Pinky Parkinson

finds out." Fliplugs' tone was a mixture of horror and glee. He was delighted to be involved in a calamity for which somebody else would have to take the blame. "You don't know old Pinky! He'll do his nut! He'll blow his top! He'll jettison his booster! It takes days and days to fill the bath, because it all has to be warmed up as it goes in. And it costs the earth to heat it. Pounds and pounds!"

"I'm terribly sorry. I never meant—"

"No good being sorry to me. *I* don't have to pay for it," the boy went on. "But you'll have to own up before you go, otherwise he may think one of our chaps did it."

Jennings was taut with apprehension. It would be bad enough trying to explain away an accident like this at his own school, but the prospect of confessing to some strange master renowned for blowing his top and jettisoning his booster was enough to make the mind boggle with panic: particularly with Mr. Wilkins standing by, rigid with embarrassment and planning unspeakable punishments to follow when they got back to school.

The boy squared his shoulders and clutched at a straw of hope. "Perhaps it hasn't all poured out yet. Perhaps we could stop it, if we go right away."

"Well, it's out of bounds by rights," Fliplugs demurred, "but I suppose we could risk it, seeing that it's an emergency."

So saying, he led the way out through the front door and across the playground with Jennings following hard on his heels.

The Linbury coach was waiting a few yards down the drive with its lights on, and Jennings noticed that his colleagues had already taken their seats for the homeward journey. Mr. Hind, also, was aboard, and Mr. Wilkins was standing beside the vehicle straining his eyes into the dusk in search of the one passenger who had not yet arrived.

Jennings shrank into the cover of Fliplugs' shadow and closed up on him, so that the taller boy would shield him from the master's line of vision. Whatever happened later, an inspection of the swimming bath was the first thing to be done.

The sports hall was in darkness as the boys approached, but the building was unlocked and they slipped inside and made their way along the corridor. The door to the swimming bath was on their right. Fliplugs pushed it open and switched on the light. . . .

The bath was empty!

Fliplugs winced and screwed up his face in mock anguish. "Whew! You've done it this time, old friend! You've made a right royal carve-up and no mistake. Wait till you get a bill for heating half a million gallons of water at five pence a unit—or whatever it is. Wait till—"

"All right, all right! You needn't go on about it," Jennings broke in. He stared at the empty pool with unbelieving eyes. There'd be the most frightful row when he owned up. Accident or not, what he'd done was unforgivable.

Numb with misery, he turned and made his way back to the entrance of the building, with Fliplugs skipping beside him prophesying the horrors in store for people foolish enough to interfere with stop-cocks which they didn't understand.

Mr. Wilkins spotted the boys as they emerged from the sports hall.

"Jennings!" he boomed in a voice of thunder. "Come

here at once! Quickly, boy, quickly! How much longer are you going to keep us waiting!"

Jennings scuttled across the tarmac and skidded to a halt beside the coach.

"Where on earth have you been?" Mr. Wilkins stormed. "We've been waiting for ten minutes. Get in the coach at once!"

The boy hesitated, uncertain how to explain.

"Well, sir, I'm not actually quite ready to come yet, sir," he faltered. "It wouldn't be fair to the Bracebridge chaps because they might have to take the blame."

Mr. Wilkins stared at the ill-shod figure in bewilderment. "Take the blame! What on earth are you talking about?"

"Well, unfortunately, sir, something terrible's happened," Jennings began. "I was trying to warm up the shower bath water with a little wheel thing I'd found, and quite by chance I—sort of—accidentally emptied the swimming bath by mistake."

"You did *what*!"

"Emptied the swimming bath, sir. It's all gone down the spout. It was an absolute accident, of course. There was this little wheel thing, you see, and when I turned it the water ran out."

"Thousands and thousands of gallons all pouring to waste," added Fliplugs, anxious that Mr. Wilkins should appreciate the full extent of the disaster. "All steamed up to eighty degrees Fahrenheit at enormous expense. And it costs pounds and pounds to heat it up from cold."

For a moment Mr. Wilkins was speechless, and Fliplugs (a keen scientist) seized the chance to explain the technical details in terms which even a slow-witted grown-up could understand.

"It's like pulling the plug out of a wash-basin, you see," he went on. "Except that, instead of a little rubber stopper at the end of a chain, there's a wheel-valve with a sluice gate and—"

But Mr. Wilkins' keen brain needed no scientific explanation. The facts were clear enough.

"This is outrageous!" he cried as soon as the power of speech returned. "You—you stupid boy, Jennings. Why in the name of reason did you do a thing like that?"

"It was a mistake, sir. I told you. The water was cold and I thought—"

"Yes, yes, yes, but why choose Bracebridge of all places!" Like Jennings ten minutes earlier, Mr. Wilkins went hot and cold at the prospect of admitting responsibility for such fantastic behaviour. What on earth would Mr. Parkinson think of a visiting team which caused such a costly accident? What on earth would he think of the master in charge of them? "Just wait till we get back to school," he threatened. "Your conduct is past belief. We shall have to find Mr. Parkinson at once and tell him what you've done."

But their quest was unnecessary, for just then their host came strolling across the tarmac to bid farewell to his guests. "Just off, eh!" he said genially.

Mr. Wilkins returned the genial smile with a sickly grin. "I say, Parkinson, I'm terribly sorry but there's been a slight—er—an unfortunate accident. This wretched boy here has done something unbelievably stupid. He's let your bath water run away."

Mr. Parkinson looked puzzled. "My bath water! But I'm not taking a bath—not now, anyway. I'm just going to take prep."

"No, no. Not an *ordinary* bath—the swimming bath.

He tells me he found a little wheel, so he turned it. And now, it seems, he's emptied the pool. I'll make sure he's severely punished, of course, and naturally we shall defray the cost of the heating when you've filled it up again."

Mr. Parkinson's expression had been growing more and more puzzled as the explanation proceeded. He pursed his lips, shooting the points of his moustache forward like an elephant's tusks. Then he said: "I don't understand this at all. What makes you think this boy has emptied the swimming bath?"

"Oh, but I did, sir," Jennings confessed. "I didn't mean to. It just happened."

"Yes, that's quite right, sir," confirmed Fliplugs, who had been hovering within earshot, agog with excitement. It was not that he bore the culprit any ill-will, but if the poor wretch was going to be torn limb from limb in any case, Fliplugs didn't want to miss the performance. "We've just been over to have a look. There isn't a drop of water left. The bath's completely empty."

Mr. Parkinson nodded. "Of *course* it's empty. I had it drained for the winter a couple of days ago." He frowned at his pupil. "You obviously weren't listening during assembly on Thursday, Hodges, when I announced that there wouldn't be any more swimming this term."

Hodges, *alias* Fliplugs, leaped like a mountain goat. His hand shot to his mouth in sudden realisation.

"Oh, my goodness! Yes, of course. So you did, sir. I'd forgotten all about it."

"Forgotten!"

"Yes, sir, but I remember now. Ever so clearly. No more swimming, you said."

Jennings rocked on his heels with surprise. "You mean I didn't empty it after all," he gasped. "Wow! Thank goodness for that."

"Ah, but you *would* have done, if it'd been full," said Fliplugs, unwilling to admit defeat.

Jennings' face was suffused with a broad, beaming smile as he swung round on Mr. Wilkins and said: "Hear that, sir! Super, isn't it. Lucky old me!"

Despite his relief, Mr. Wilkins was still seething with annoyance. His dignity had suffered. Jennings had been a nuisance and an embarrassment ever since they had arrived.

He glowered at the boy and said: "Get in the coach, Jennings, and report to me when we get back. You've caused more than enough trouble for one afternoon."

CHAPTER 5

Aerosol Accident

Mr. CARTER was marking books in the staff room when the teams arrived back from Bracebridge. He heard the coach drive up, the scuttle of feet as the passengers alighted, and then the sound of Venables' penetrating voice broadcasting the results of the matches to the heads leaning out of the common-room window, demanding to know how the teams had fared.

A few minutes later Mr. Wilkins came into the staff room and slumped into an armchair.

"I'm exhausted," he announced. "I've had a somewhat trying afternoon—thanks to young Master Jennings. How did you get on?"

"We lost, 2–1," Mr. Carter replied. "And we also had a somewhat trying afternoon—thanks to L. P. Wilkins, Esq."

"Thanks to me!" Mr. Wilkins sat bolt upright. "What on earth do you mean?"

"Your information that the pavilion key was on a key-ring in your room proved to be wrong—it wasn't! And as the Head had gone off in his car with one of the spare keys, and the odd-job man had gone off duty with the other, we were in real trouble. We had to break a window in order to get in."

"But that's ridiculous. Of *course* it was in my room," Mr. Wilkins maintained. "I distinctly remember making sure it was there before lunch."

"Well, it wasn't there *after* lunch," his colleague

pointed out. "And to make matters worse, the Brace-bridge team arrived while we were still running round trying to find a duplicate, so we couldn't let them in to change."

"Yes, but I distinctly remember—"

"And as if that wasn't bad enough, we had no foot-balls and no corner flags." Mr. Carter shook his head in reproach. "It really is too bad of you, Wilkins, to make these wildly irresponsible statements without bothering to make sure of your facts. The headmaster sounded most annoyed about the broken window when he got back."

"It *must* be on my key-ring. You can't have looked properly." Mr. Wilkins jumped to his feet and made for the door. "I'll go and have a look myself."

When he reached the sitting-room on the second floor he found Jennings standing outside the door. It was, perhaps, unfortunate that Mr. Wilkins did not arrive a few minutes later, for by then his caller would have had time to slip into the room unobserved and return the missing key.

As it was, Jennings heard the approaching footsteps just in time and decided to postpone his mission until the coast was clear. Accordingly, he put the key back in his pocket and switched his mind over to the other reason for his visit.

"Ah, there you are, sir," he said. "You told me to report to you when we got back."

Mr. Wilkins grunted in reply and strode into the room, leaving his caller outside in the corridor. He made straight for the hook by the window and sorted through his keys. His front door key was there, and his car ignition key, and several more: but the key of the pavilion was missing.

It was extraordinary! He was sure he had seen it that morning. But then, he reflected, thinking of his visitor outside the door, he was equally sure that he had put Jennings' watch in the pocket of his old sports jacket the previous week. He must be getting absent-minded! Perhaps the strain of teaching Form 3 for fourteen lessons a week was beginning to tell!

He crossed to the door and beckoned the boy into the room. Then he said: "Now listen to me, Jennings. Your behaviour this afternoon was wildly irresponsible. You let the school down badly, and I will not tolerate such conduct in future."

"Yes, sir . . . No, sir," Jennings said earnestly. He could see the key-ring on the hook behind Mr. Wilkins' left shoulder. If only the master had come upstairs a few minutes later! If only he could be called away to the telephone! . . . But this was mere wishful thinking. Dutifully, he switched his mind back to what Mr. Wilkins was saying, and tried to make sense of the spate of words bouncing off his ear-drums.

For ten minutes Mr. Wilkins spoke sternly on the subject of immature behaviour, illustrating his argument with reference to people who went to neighbouring schools in bizarre footwear and interfered with the plumbing when they got there. Jennings said: "Yes, sir. . . . No, sir," at intervals, and promised to behave better in future.

When the lecture had run its course, Mr. Wilkins dropped his reprimanding tone of voice and said: "One other thing, Jennings: that wrist-watch that you asked me to look after. It's quite safe, of course, but just at the moment, unfortunately, I can't quite remember where I put it."

"Oh, that's all right, sir," the boy assured him. "It isn't a valuable one."

"That's not the point. Valuable or not, you left it in my keeping and I shall certainly return it in good order. It's just that you'll have to be patient until I get a chance to have a proper look for it."

"Yes, sir. I'll be patient, sir. That's all right, sir."

Jennings departed, relieved to have been let off so lightly. Old Wilkie's temper must have cooled down a bit on the homeward journey, he thought. He wasn't greatly worried about returning the pavilion key either. There'd be plenty of chances during the next few days, if he kept his eyes open!

In the dormitory that evening, Darbishire had a few serious words to say on the subject of Bonfire Night celebrations.

"I hope you realise that there's less than a fortnight to go," he told Jennings as they stood at the wash-basins together. "What about all those famous plans of yours for asking people to the fireworks and taking a collection?"

"Yes, and what about your famous scheme for making a guy and taking it round the village?" demanded Atkinson from his bed by the door. "*That's* going to take a bit of organising if it's going to be done without the masters finding out."

Jennings was able to report that, in some respects, the plans were already taking shape. Martin-Jones (Hon. Sec.) had already drawn up a list of the fireworks to be bought with the proceeds of the Form 3 Firework Fund, and Mr. Carter had agreed to invite several local residents to attend the celebrations.

"He's going to get a bunch of old geezers like Miss

Thorpe and Dr. Furnival and the vicar to come along,"
Jennings told them. "That ought to step up the collection for his famous worthy cause."

"But that's only three," Atkinson objected. "The
best thing to do would be to shoot a flaming rocket
through the library window. Then we'd have the
whole of the Dunhambury Fire Brigade here and we
could pass the hat round to them as well."

Atkinson's suggestion was rejected as unpractical,
and as soon as the boys were in bed, they settled down
to discuss the more serious aspects of the scheme.

"We ought to have a committee to make sure things
get done properly," Jennings decided. "Martin-Jones
and his bunch are looking after the fireworks, but
there's really nobody in charge of the guy—well, not
officially."

"How about us five, then?" said Darbishire. "We
could call ourselves the Special Action Sub-committee
of the Form 3 Firework Fund. We'd be a sort of ginger-
group, if you know what I mean."

"Good scheme," said Temple. "Hands up all who
agree."

The resolution was carried by five votes to nil and
the ginger-group got down to work without delay.

There should be no difficulty in finding materials
for making a guy, they decided. Robinson, the school
cleaner, was known to have a pile of old sacks and
some bales of straw in his tool-shed. If asked politely,
he could hardly refuse to give the boys what they
needed for constructing a suitable body and limbs.

It would then be Matron's privilege to provide
trousers, jacket, hat and boots from the stock of discarded clothes which she kept in a cupboard in the
sewing-room.

"I saw some decent Guy Fawkes masks in Dunham-bury when we went through this afternoon," Jennings informed the group. "If anybody's going into town we could ask them to get us one."

After some argument it was decided that Venables and Temple should be responsible for contacting Robinson and making the guy's body, while Jennings and Darbishire should select some stylish garments in which to clothe it.

So far, the arrangements seemed simple enough, but it was agreed that problems might arise over the question of smuggling the effigy off the school premises and taking a collection in the village street.

Darbishire was in favour of asking permission to do this openly, but Jennings objected on the grounds that the request might well be refused—even although it was in support of a worthy cause.

"Supposing we run into the Head or somebody while we're taking the collection," he argued. "We could always say we thought it would be all right, as it was for charity. But think what a frantic hoo-hah there'd be if we got copped after they'd said we weren't to do it."

The argument seemed reasonable, so they agreed that the fund-raising expedition should be carried out under a veil of strict secrecy. At the same time, they wanted everybody to know that a guy was to be one of the attractions of Bonfire Night, and with this object in view, Atkinson was appointed to the rank of Public Relations Officer to G. Fawkes, Esq. (deceased).

During the next few days Venables and Temple completed their share of the project as far as they could. Robinson gave them a large potato sack which they filled with straw and coaxed and pummelled into

a fair resemblance of a human head and torso. After
that they could do no more until Jennings and Darbishire had fulfilled their share of the contract.

"How much longer have we got to go on waiting for
his clothes?" Temple complained to Jennings after tea
on Sunday. "We can't even make his legs until we've
got his trousers to stuff the straw into."

But the men's outfitting department was chafing under
a frustrating delay. "It's all Matron's fault," Jennings
complained bitterly. "Women! Tut! They don't seem
to understand things like ordinary human beings."

Matron was a young, attractive nursing-sister whose
main responsibility was the health of the boys in her
charge. But as, in addition, she supervised the work of
the sewing-room, any request for cast-off garments had
to be made to her.

"I've asked her about a million times," Jennings
went on. "She says we can have some old clothes, but
we've got to wait till she's had time to sort them out."

"Tell her to get a move on, then," Temple urged.
"We want to have it all ready to trundle round the
village by next Saturday."

"Ah, but she doesn't know about that," Jennings
pointed out. "She thinks we shan't be needing it until
November 5th, and I can't say anything about the
village trip because it's on the secret list."

Temple pulled a long face. "Well, don't leave it too
long, then. Have another bash at her tomorrow."

Jennings and Darbishire were waiting outside the
door when Matron arrived at the dispensary on
Monday morning.

"I haven't forgotten your guy," she told them, leading the way into the room. "I'll look something out for
you one day this week."

"But it's urgent, Matron. We want to get it finished and you're holding up production," Jennings insisted.

Darbishire gave her a winning smile and said: "You needn't actually bother to choose the clothes yourself, Matron. You just give us permission and we'll have a little rootle through the cupboard and pick out what we need."

Matron could imagine the state that the cupboard would be in after the boys had finished their "little rootle".

"I'm not having the sewing-room looking like a bull-fight at a jumble sale," she said firmly. "Come and see me on Wednesday afternoon and I'll fix you up. But don't—I repeat, *don't*—touch anything unless I'm there, or you'll find yourselves in *real* trouble."

"Yes, Matron. Of course, Matron. Thank you very much, Matron."

The boys were about to leave when she called Jennings back and stared with mild horror at the untidy mop of hair fringing his eyes like a tasselled lampshade.

"I put your name on the hairdresser's list last week," she said. "Why didn't you have it cut when Mr. Hales was here?"

Jennings hesitated, not caring to admit that his object in evading the hairdresser ever since the beginning of term was because he wanted to find out how long his hair would grow.

"I—er—I was very busy doing my stamp-album last Tuesday, Matron, and by the time I got down to the changing-room it was too late. He'd packed up and gone home."

She frowned with suspicion. "And the time before?"

The boy searched his mind for an excuse. "Well, I'd

got a bit of a cold, you see, and I thought if the hair-dresser started hacking off great chunks and the weather turned frosty, I might catch—"

Matron's laugh drowned the rest of his excuse. "I've heard some tall stories in my time, but this is past anyone's belief. Anyway, I'm not having you going around looking like an Old English sheepdog just so that you can claim the Form 3 record for dodging the barber. I'll see you don't get away with it next time he comes."

The length of Jennings' hair was a topic of conversation during staff supper that evening.

"It's appalling," the headmaster said as he helped himself to the gravy. "It's over his collar. It'll be half-way down his back if something isn't done about it very soon."

"I've threatened to cut it for him myself," said Mr. Wilkins. "He looks like a yak."

Generously, Matron played down the real reason for Jennings' aversion to the barber's scissors. "I've put him on the list every time, but he always seems to be otherwise engaged," she said. "Unfortunately, the hair-dresser won't be coming again for nearly a fortnight, so—"

"A fortnight!" Mr. Pemberton-Oakes was horrified. "I'm not putting up with a walking haystack in my class for two more weeks." He frowned and shook his head. "We shall have to make other arrangements. I shall send him to Dunhambury on the bus next half-holiday and make sure he tells the hairdresser to give him a good, short crop."

Mr. Wilkins nodded approvingly and ran his finger round the inside of his collar. He, too, could do with a slight trim, he reflected.

The weather turned wet on Wednesday and football practice was cancelled. Shortly before two o'clock when the school settled down to spend the half-holiday in quiet, indoor occupations, Jennings and Darbishire hurried off to the sewing-room for their appointment with Matron.

There was no answer to their knock for she was not expecting them so early, and for some while they waited in the corridor, perched on a laundry hamper and drumming their feet against its wickerwork sides.

Bromwich passed by and said: "If you're waiting for Matron, you'd better send out for sandwiches and sleeping-bags. She'll be hours yet. She's gone down to the village in Mr. Carter's car."

Jennings was disgusted. "Tut! Women! Sabotage, that's what it is. She promised faithfully she'd see us this afternoon."

"She probably meant after football. She didn't know it was going to be cancelled," Darbishire pointed out. "Might as well push off and come back at four o'clock."

But they had no other plans so they stayed where they were, restless, aimless and bored. After a while, Jennings said: "Let's go in and have a squint through the cupboard and see what sort of clobber she's got there."

"She said we weren't to touch anything," Darbishire objected. "We're supposed to wait out here till she comes."

"I'm not *going* to touch anything, you clodpoll. Just have a look, that's all. It's quite safe. If she's not expecting us till after football, she won't be here for hours."

Jennings rattled the handle, but the door was secured by a Yale-type lock and wouldn't open. For some moments he stood frowning at the panels and then—purely as an experiment and with no thought of success—he produced the pavilion key from his pocket and inserted it in the lock.

The door swung open.

Darbishire was astounded. "Hey, where did you get that key?" he demanded.

"It's the key of the pav—the one everyone's looking for," Jennings explained. "I borrowed it without per the day we went to Bracebridge."

"Wow! You'd better watch out. The Head said in Assembly that if anybody found it they were—"

"I know, I heard him. I've been trying to get it back on to Old Wilkie's key-ring, but it's not in his room any more. I reckon he must carry it about in his pocket."

Still puzzled, Darbishire said: "But if it's the key of the pav, why does it fit the sewing-room?"

Jennings shrugged. "Cheap old school locks, I suppose. One key fits the tinny old lot." Smiling, he slipped the key back in his pocket. "Useful bit of information, that! Worth knowing!"

He led the way into the sewing-room. Darbishire pattered in nervously after him, fearful of Matron's premature arrival.

The discarded clothes, together with some theatrical costumes from by-gone plays and concerts, were stored in a built-in cupboard stretching from floor to ceiling. Jennings turned the catch, and as the door swung open a bundle of nondescript garments dropped down on to the floor.

Darbishire hopped from foot to foot in apprehension. "Put them back quickly," he urged. "She mustn't know we've been rootling about in here, or she won't give us anything for the guy. She said so."

Jennings replaced the bundle. Then, on top of an old pair of jeans on the shelf above, he caught sight of a pile of silver-coloured cardboard breast-plates left over from a Shakespearean production.

"Hey, look at these," he said, taking out one of the breast-plates and holding it up for his friend's inspection. "These are the ones Matron made for us when we did that chunk out of *Henry V*. Remember?"

Darbishire remembered and shivered in retrospect. Thanks to Jennings, the performance had been the sort of nightmare that would remain in his memory for years to come.*

By now, Jennings was delving into the theatrical wardrobe uttering cries of recognition as he identified properties and costumes from his historic production.

A few seconds later he withdrew his head and turned to his friend holding aloft an aerosol spray of aluminium paint.

"How about this, then! I've found Matron's atomiser," he announced.

Darbishire glanced at it and said: "She couldn't split the atom with a thing like that. She'd need a special sort of power station."

"Very funny! Hilarious!" Jennings said scathingly. "What I mea ;, this is the spray-gun gadget that she used to paint our armour-plating for the play." He shook the tin, which still appeared to contain a fair amount of liquid. "They're super—these gadgets! You don't need a paint brush. You only have to press the button." He propped the cardboard breast-plate on the window-sill and took aim. "Like this, look."

"You don't want to paint it again—not *now*," Darbi-

*See *Our Friend Jennings*

shire demurred. "Supposing Matron comes in and finds it all wet."

"It won't be. This spray stuff dries at once. Look, I'll prove it."

There were instructions printed on the tin, and a warning stressing the importance of pointing the nozzle carefully in the required direction. But Jennings was in no mood to waste time with warnings. Standing back from his target and holding the canister head high, he pressed the button on the top.

The result was disastrous. For instead of spraying the target, the jet shot from the nozzle in the reverse direction, coating the marksman's hair with a stream of aluminium paint.

It was all over in a split-second. By the time Jennings had jerked his finger off the spray-button his head was shining with a silver luminosity.

"Wow! That was a near one," he remarked as he put down the canister. "I nearly got a squirt in the eye, then. Lucky it missed."

It was clear from his light-hearted tone that he had no idea that anything unusual had happened. But the look of horror on Darbishire's face and the note of panic in his voice told him that something was amiss.

"*Missed! Nearly* got a squirt!" Darbishire echoed. "What d'you mean—*nearly* got a squirt! You got the whole operation from blast-off to splash-down all over your great bonce. . . . Look at your head! Look at your hair! . . . . It's plastered!"

There was a mirror on the opposite wall and Jennings raced across the room to confirm the extent of the damage.

He gasped in dismay at the sight of his reflection. . . . His hair was a matted wig of silver-grey rats' tails. He

touched it and found his fingers smeared with aluminium paint.

"Oh, gosh, this is frightful!" he cried.

"You must be mad," Darbishire gibbered in exas-
piration. "Fancy pointing it straight at your head
and—"

"I didn't *know* it was pointing at me. I thought it was
pointing the other way. It's only a titchy little nozzle
the size of a pin-hole and you can't see it properly
unless you—"

"Never mind the excuses. Let's get out of here and
get your hair washed before Matron turns up," Darbishire urged.

In frantic haste they replaced the cardboard breast-
plates, closed the cupboard and scuttled out into the
corridor, slamming the door shut behind them.

CHAPTER 6

Short Back and Sides

THE FUGITIVES were careful not to be seen on their way downstairs to the wash-room, and Darbishire went in front keeping a look-out for approaching masters at every bend and corner.

As they reached the ground floor, a thought occurred to him and he said: "Perhaps it won't wash off, Jen. If it's a decent sort of paint, it'll need a blow-lamp to shift it, now that it's dry."

"Huh! I'm not having my head sizzled with a blow-lamp, thank you very much."

"Or you may have to shave it. Unless, of course, you can make the Head believe that Old Wilkie's gruesome maths lessons have turned your hair grey all of a sudden."

Jennings snorted. The situation was worrying enough to turn *anyone's* hair grey, he thought—without having to listen to old Darbi trying to be funny about it! He hurried into the wash-room and stopped in front of the basins.

"I hope to goodness it *will* wash out," he said, peering at his reflection in the mirror. "If Matron finds out, she'll know we disobeyed her orders about going to the cupboard when she wasn't there. And that means she won't give us any clothes for the guy."

Darbishire poked his head through a roller-towel and twisted it into a turban. "That isn't all it means—

not by a long chalk," he replied. "It could be a hundred times worse."

"Worse? . . . How?"

"Because the first thing she'll ask you is how we got into the sewing-room. And you'll have to tell her how you went into Old Wilkie's room when he wasn't there and filched the key of the pav—the key every body in the school has been searching for since last week."

Jennings' expression was grave as he filled the basin and reached for the carbolic soap. "You're dead right, Darbi," he said grimly. "Let's get on with my shampoo quickly and keep our fingers crossed."

The carbolic soap shampoo was a complete failure. In spite of the most vigorous scalp massage, the aluminium coating all over Jennings' head was glowing as brightly as ever when the cleansing operation was abandoned a few minutes later.

"It's hopeless. The soap just seems to make it stick harder than ever," he complained, dabbing his dripping locks with a roller-towel.

"We'll have to cut it off, then," Darbishire decided. "Wait here while I go and fetch my nail scissors."

He scampered off to the dormitory on his errand and was soon back again, ready to try his hand. But Darbishire's efforts with his blunt, curved scissors turned a bad situation into a worse one. After a few patches of hair had been snipped off at random, the surface of Jennings' head began to look like a moth-eaten hearthbrush.

"Hey, that's enough! Pack it up, for goodness' sake," the victim protested, backing away from the amateur barber and inspecting the damage in the mirror. "You've done it all lop-sided, you clumsy clodpoll.

There'll be the most frantic hoo-hah when Matron sees it."

"I was only trying to help. I'm not an expert," Darbishire defended himself.

Even so, he was forced to admit that his contribution had done more harm than good. For there was now a bald patch over Jennings' left ear and jagged doorsteps of hair leading up to the top of his head: his fringe was gap-toothed and the back of his neck looked like a map of the west coast of Scotland . . . But the aluminium paint still glowed as brightly as before.

Jennings stopped glowering at himself in the mirror and glanced up at the wash-room clock. It was twenty minutes past three. "If only I could get into Dunhambury without anybody seeing, I could go to the hairdressers and let them have a go," he said.

Darbishire nodded, thankful to be relieved of his task. "Good scheme! Ask for Mr. Hales—the chap who comes here to do our haircuts. He's probably got a special shampoo with paint-remover in it for cases like yours. And he could give you a short back-and-sides afterwards to smooth out the parts I've left a bit bumpy."

"That'd give the game away," Jennings objected. "I don't want it to *look* as though I've had a haircut, or the masters might spot it. Just a slight trim, that's all."

"Ah, yes, but that all depends on whether—"

"Stop nattering, Darbi," Jennings said sternly. "I'm trying to work out a plan."

It was well known amongst his friends at Linbury Court that whenever Jennings conceived a plan to outwit authority, it was sure to be carefully thought out and entirely practical—*on paper*! Details concerning time, place, excuses, methods of transport, disguise (if any), provisions and equipment were worked out with such care that all the conspirators involved could look forward with confidence to a successful outcome. . . . It was only when the plan was actually in operation that some unexpected snag or blow of fate beyond the planner's control tended to throw the project into confusion.

The Plan of the Secret Haircut © Copyright by *J. C. T. Jennings* was no exception. In theory, it appeared foolproof and showed a planning ability worthy of a military commander.

The first problem was how to get out of the school grounds without being observed by a master. As usual, Jennings cleared this hurdle with his customary flair for intrigue.

It had stopped raining by now; and at a quarter to four the day boys who had stayed on to take part in indoor hobbies would be departing by bicycle or on foot. Among them would be Pettigrew, a plump, freckle-faced third-former who cycled to school each day along the Dunhambury road.

In contrast to his fellows who wore navy-blue school raincoats, Pettigrew arrived at school on wet days in a bright yellow plastic mackintosh: and it was this vivid, eye-catching garment that Jennings decided to make use of, by way of a disguise.

"Go and ask Petters if he'll lend it to me to go down the drive in, and say I'll meet him in the bike shed at twenty-to-four," Jennings instructed his henchman when he had finished outlining his plan. "And get my cap on your way back. I daren't put my head outside the door without something to cover it up."

"Yes, but I don't quite see how you're going to—"

"Don't panic, Darbi. If only I can get past the front

steps without being spotted, the rest of the plan should be plain sailing."

And, indeed, this looked like being the case. According to timetable, Jennings proposed catching the four o'clock bus into Dunhambury. He would be at the hairdressers well before the half-hour, and out again in time to catch the 5.30 bus for the return journey. He had enough money for his fare, but probably not quite enough to cover the cost of a haircut and shampoo.

However, Mr. Hales, the school hairdresser, always seemed an obliging sort of man on his visits to Linbury Court and would, no doubt, agree to send the bill for his services to his customer's parents at their home address.

Darbishire returned a few minutes later to announce that Pettigrew and his friends were willing to co-operate in the first stage of the plan.

"He says you can have the mac and the bike so long as you leave them just outside the main gate for when he gets there," he reported, tossing Jennings' school cap into an empty wash-basin. "I've got some day boys lined up for your bodyguard past the front steps. Only, watch it, for Pete's sake. Mr. Hind's on duty and he's got eyes like an electric scanner."

The clock on the wash-room wall stood at twenty-five minutes to four. Time to stand by for action! Jennings put on his cap and pulled it down firmly.

"Better not meet a master between here and the bike shed," Darbishire cautioned. "He might think it a bit funny if he saw you with your cap on indoors."

Jennings had already thought of that. He would leave by the wash-room window, he decided, and take cover from the laurel bushes bordering the path to the bicycle shed.

A small precaution, perhaps, but typical of the master-planner's methods. Nobody could deny that Jennings' schemes were foolproof down to the smallest detail—well, in theory, anyway!

Mr. Hind stood at the top of the steps outside the main entrance, puffing at his cherrywood pipe and holding the day boys' attendance register under his arm. As master on duty, it was his task to make sure that the day boys went home in an orderly manner and at the proper time.

There was never any ceremony about this: the boys merely raised their caps as they walked or cycled past the front steps, while the duty master checked off their names on his list.

As a rule, the cyclists departed singly or in pairs, but today they appeared in close formation. As they swirled past the steps, Mr. Hind noticed Marshall and Lewis on the outside, flanking a tightly packed group, in the middle of which Pettigrew's yellow mackintosh stood out like a beacon in a black-out.

The riders raised their caps as they passed the steps, though a close observer might have noticed that the boy in the yellow mackintosh averted his face and merely tweaked the peak of his headgear. This wasn't the moment, Jennings felt, to risk exposing his silvery locks to the public gaze.

Mr. Hind placed a tick against the names in the register: Marshall, Lewis, Pettigrew—and the rest. He had no difficulty in marking his list in spite of the tight huddle of machines in the cyclists' convoy.

When the last of the day boys had gone home, the duty master made his way to the staff room and stood by the window drinking a cup of tea. Suddenly he put down his cup and said: "Good heavens, I'm seeing things!"

Mr. Carter and Matron, who were chatting together by the tea trolley, looked round in surprise.

"I've just seen Pettigrew walk past the window," Mr. Hind proclaimed, as though announcing the appearance of a little green man from Outer Space.

"Well, why not?" asked Matron. "It's time the day boys went home, isn't it?"

"But he's gone home already! I saw him cycling down the drive some minutes ago. I ticked him off my list."

"You must have made a mistake."

"Mistake! You can't mistake that lifeboat-launching yellow mackintosh. You can tell it a mile off. I don't understand this at all."

Mr. Hind opened the window and shouted after the retreating figure: but by this time Pettigrew was round the corner of the building, out of sight and out of earshot.

"Extraordinary!" the master observed as he closed the window. It was most mysterious! Either his eyesight or his imagination must be playing him tricks . . . Or perhaps the strain of teaching Art to Form 3 was beginning to tell!

Matron finished her tea and said: "Well, I must be off. I've promised to go through the sewing-room cupboard with Jennings and Darbishire to choose some clothes for their guy. I expect they'll be waiting for me."

As she turned to go, she noticed a spare cup and saucer on the trolley and added: "I see Mr. Wilkins hasn't been in for a cup of tea. Most unusual! Has he gone out, do you know?"

Mr. Carter helped himself to a biscuit. "I think so,"

he replied. "He said something about popping into Dunhambury for a haircut, if he'd got time."

It was not part of Jennings' plan that Pettigrew should be seen by a master when passing the staff-room window. This was a mere error of timing on the day boy's part and had nothing to do with the overall plan, which had now progressed to Stage Two of the operation.

When he reached the main road, Pettigrew found his bicycle with the yellow mackintosh draped over the handlebars. As arranged, the machine was partly concealed in the hedge near the bus stop. There was no sign of Jennings, for the four o'clock bus had left some minutes before, and by this time the master-planner was nearly halfway to Dunhambury.

The day boy put on his mackintosh and set off for home. It was all very well for the boarders to concoct these famous schemes, he said to himself as he pedalled along the road, but where would they be without the day boys to help in carrying them out!

Jennings got off the bus at the stop near the traffic lights in the High Street. There were at least three men's hairdressing saloons that he knew of in Dunhambury, but he had no means of telling at which one Mr. Hales was employed. The nearest was down the hill from the traffic lights, so he hurried back along the main street and poked his head round the shop door. But there was no sign of Mr. Hales, so he decided to try a more prosperous-looking saloon which he remembered having seen on the opposite side of the road.

He made his way past the supermarket, where the windows were so curtained with advertising posters that it was impossible to glimpse the range of goods on sale within. He didn't stop at the music shop (*£5 and upwards offered for your old piano*), but the display of Guy Fawkes' masks in the newsagent's next door brought him to an abrupt halt.

They needed a mask for the guy, and this might be his only chance of obtaining one in time for the secret money-raising demonstration in the village planned for the following Saturday.

The masks were so grotesque and so ugly that they bore little resemblance to the average human face, and none at all to the features of the original G. Fawkes, Esq. (deceased). But Jennings was not fussy about historical detail and decided that a monstrous plastic mask with a bulbous red nose and drooping walrus moustache in the centre of the display would be ideal for his purpose.

He hurried into the shop, bought the plastic monstrosity, stuffed it into his pocket and rushed out again. The ten pence it had cost him would upset his hairdressing budget, he realised, as he went on up the hill; he would just *have* to persuade Mr. Hales to send the bill on to his parents.

An electric sign in the shape of a rotating barber's pole was displaying its message a few yards up the street. Beneath the sign the fascia board said: *Walton's Men's Hairdressing Saloon* (*Established* 1929). Jennings hastened towards it, pushed open the saloon door and looked inside.

The shop was long and rather narrow. Mirrors and wash-basins stretched the length of the wall down one side of the room where four assistants were tending the needs of their clients. Along the opposite wall were leather-covered benches occupied by customers awaiting attention.

Jennings' spirits rose as he spotted Mr. Hales at work at the far end of the shop. So he had found the right place! He walked past the waiting customers and sat down on the bench behind Mr. Hales' chair.

He did not have long to wait. Indeed, his turn came before the school hairdresser was free, but he declined the offer of another chair, preferring to wait for the assistant of his choice.

A few moments later, Mr. Hales helped an elderly customer on with his coat and turned to the benches behind him. "Who's next?" he demanded briskly.

Jennings hurried forward and took his seat, his cap still planted firmly on his head.

"Good afternoon, Mr. Hales. You know me, don't you?" he said uneasily. "My name's Jennings from Linbury Court and I've come to see you because of—er—what you might call a sort of emergency."

The hairdresser nodded. He was a pleasant, white-haired man in spectacles who had been attending the school on alternate Tuesday evenings for a number of years. It was not often that any of the pupils came into the shop, although on rare occasions the headmaster might send along a boy whose hair needed trimming for some special occasion.

"Emergency haircut, eh!" Mr. Hales observed. "That's okay, son. Only, I might get on a bit better if you took your cap off!"

The customer hesitated. "Well, that's just it! That's the emergency, if you see what I mean. I've had an accident with a tin of paint." He removed his cap and gave a little nervous laugh.

Mr. Hales wasn't prepared for the shock. He recoiled, wincing and pursing his lips at the sight that met his eyes.

"Cor! What a mess! That's a right creamer, if ever I saw one. What happened, son? You look like a thorn-bush in a blizzard."

Jennings outlined the facts of the disaster. And then, as Mr. Hales seemed such an understanding sort of man, he told him of his predicament and explained why this had to be a secret hairdressing operation, of which no word must ever reach the ears of the masters.

To the boy's surprise, Mr. Hales seemed to find the incident funny. He laughed so much that he could hardly hold the clippers steady as he made good the ravages of Darbishire's handiwork with the nail scissors. "Next time your pal gives you a haircut, tell him to use a meat axe," he suggested, quaking with inward laughter.

However, he proved to be a staunch ally, despite his flippant remarks. For he promised to respect Jennings' security arrangements and even waived his claim to immediate payment when he heard of his customer's financial crisis.

"That's all right, son. No need to write to your parents," he said. "I'll just charge up one more haircut when I send the school account in at the end of term."

"Thanks awfully. That's ever so decent of you," replied Jennings. "And you don't think Matron will find out it was me who had it done, do you?"

"Of course not. How can she, if I forget to put your name down!"

In a matter of minutes the worst features of Darbishire's bungling efforts had been toned down, and Mr. Hales set to work with a spirit shampoo to remove all traces of the aluminium paint.

The boy sat watching his reflection in the mirror as the colour gradually faded and the pile of spirit-soaked tissues and soiled cotton wool mounted round the hairdresser's ankles.

It was a pity he'd had to cut so much off, Jennings thought. He'd have to start growing his hair all over again if he was ever going to set up a record for the shaggiest head in Form 3. And besides, there was a real danger now that Matron or one of the masters would notice he had had his hair cut and demand explanations. Still, that was a risk that would have to be—

Suddenly Jennings jerked bolt upright in the chair and then shrank down again trying to conceal his face in the cape around his shoulders . . . For the shop door had swung open and, in the mirror, he could see Mr. Wilkins striding briskly into the saloon in quest of a haircut.

CHAPTER 7

In Hazard

EVEN THE MOST EXPERIENCED hairdresser can be put off his stroke by the antics of a customer who leaps like a rising trout and then wraps the barber's cape round his face as high as his ears.

"Hey, keep still! What's going on?" Mr. Hales protested. "How d'you think I can get your hair done with you wriggling about like a worm on a hook!"

Slowly and cautiously, Jennings lowered the cape just enough to expose his left eye. With this he winked a signal of warning to the baffled barber and then darted a quick glance towards the far end of the saloon.

What he saw was enough to dash the hopes of any master-planner. . . . The only customer awaiting attention was L. P. Wilkins, Esq., who was sitting on the bench just inside the door. He had picked up a magazine and was flicking through the pages.

Jennings thought hard. The fact that the master was at the far end of the shop was some consolation, for all the barbers' chairs were occupied and the assistants and their customers provided a certain amount of cover.

Not *much* cover, of course, but with a bit of luck it might be just enough to veil the identity of the shrouded figure in the farthermost chair, some thirty feet away.

But for how long? Supposing Mr. Wilkins stopped reading and started to look about him! Supposing, when his turn came, the master was shown to the chair next in line to his own! Supposing . . . .

Jennings stopped supposing: for Mr. Hales had not understood the wink of warning and was demanding explanations in a dangerously loud tone of voice.

"What's wrong, son? Ill, or something?" he was saying. "For goodness' sake, sit up and stop using the cape as a yashmak. I can't get at the back of your neck."

Keeping an eye on Mr. Wilkins' reflection in the mirror, Jennings whispered: "One of our masters. Just come in. Sitting by the door!"

"Speak up, son. That's my deaf ear on that side. *Who's* sitting on the floor?"

"No, not on the floor: by the door."

Curious to know what was happening, the hairdresser wheeled round and stared down the shop in a way that would certainly have drawn Mr. Wilkins' attention had he not been immersed in his magazine.

Jennings held his breath, but the master didn't look up and the moment of crisis passed. Mr. Hales turned back and pulled a face at his customer in the mirror.

The grimace was meant to imply that he had recognised the new arrival but couldn't do anything about it. And furthermore, that in his capacity as official hairdresser to Linbury Court School on alternate Tuesdays, he—Ronald Alfred Hales—didn't want to get involved if an awkward situation should arise between master and pupil.

Jennings sat in the barber's chair, tense with anxiety. His plan was in ruins and the outlook was hopeless. There were only a few streaks of paint left in his hair and very soon Mr. Hales would have finished his treatment.

And then what? Other customers would be coming
in and wanting his seat. So he couldn't stay where he
was. Besides, he had a bus to catch. But leaving the
shop to catch the bus would mean walking past Mr.
Wilkins!

He was still racking his brains for an answer to his
problem when one of the assistants called out: "Next
gentleman, please!" and Mr. Wilkins put down his
magazine and stepped forward to take the vacant seat.

A furtive glance showed that he was in the end chair
next to the door. But this was no help to Jennings. It
would be an act of lunacy to try to creep past him unobserved, for the mirror on the wall ruled out all hope
of escape. Mr. Wilkins had only to sit looking straight
ahead to have a perfect view of everything going on
behind his back.

Two or three customers arrived just then and sat
down on the benches to wait; and a few moments
later Mr. Hales gave Jennings' head an appraising look
and bent down and whispered: "That's it, then!
Nothing more I can do. You're on your own now,
lad."

He removed the cape from the boy's shoulders and
jerked his head towards a glass-fronted cupboard in
the corner behind him, displaying bottles of hair tonic
and tubes of shaving cream. His tone was barely
audible as he added: "Why not stand behind the showcase till he's gone! You won't be seen from the other
end of the saloon."

Jennings nodded his gratitude. He slipped out of the
chair and, sheltered by Mr. Hales who made great play
of shaking out the cape, darted across to the cupboard
and stood pressed close to the wall beside it.

From there he took stock of his plight. The showcase projected nearly two feet into the room, so if he kept still there was little chance that Mr. Wilkins would notice him. But if the showcase was his refuge it was also his prison, for he would have to stay where he was until the master had gone.

This was out of the question. He *couldn't* stay where he was—there wasn't time! He glanced at the clock on the wall halfway down the shop and saw that the hands stood at twenty-to-seven. He blinked in amazement. It couldn't be as late as that! The clock must be off its cog-wheels!

Then he blinked again and realised that the dial was on the opposite wall and he was reading the hands in the mirror. So that made the time—er—um—*wow*! Twenty minutes past five . . . And his one-and-only bus left at the half-hour. Allowing two minutes flat for a fast sprint to the bus stop, he would have to be out of the shop and on his way in eight minutes at the latest.

What were his chances? How long would Mr. Wilkins go on sitting there having his hair cut? . . . Everything depended on that!

For some while after he had watched his friend pedalling down the drive on Pettigrew's bicycle, Darbishire stood at the classroom window brooding over the weak spots in *The Plan of the Secret Haircut* © *Copyright by J. C. T. Jennings*.

The risks were considerable, he thought. On the other hand, Jennings was an old campaigner in exploits of this sort and would probably manage to muddle through somehow.

Reassured, he wandered off to the classroom to look through his stamp album, and on his way he met Matron coming down the stairs from her dispensary.

"Oh, there you are, Darbishire," she greeted him. "What happened to you and Jennings, then?"

Darbishire went rigid with guilt. She must have found out about the accident with the aerosol spray! Then he relaxed as she went on: "I thought you were both coming along to the sewing-room at four o'clock to choose some clothes for your guy. I waited nearly ten minutes for you."

"Oh, ah, yes, of course, Matron." Darbishire still felt weak at the knees, but he rallied and said: "Well, actually, we didn't know you meant four o'clock. We thought you meant after dinner, but you weren't there when we—er—went up to have a look."

"I see. Well, we could go and do it now, couldn't we! Where's Jennings?"

This was an awkward question. "He's—er—well, he isn't here, just at the moment. He's probably somewhere else—or rather, what I mean is, I don't think I can get hold of him just at the moment, if you know what I mean."

She didn't know what he meant, but she let it pass. "You'd better come and do the choosing, then. I can't waste the rest of the afternoon waiting for Jennings to put in an appearance."

She turned and led the way upstairs to the sewing-room and unlocked the door. As they went in, Darbishire looked about him anxiously, fearful that he or Jennings had left some clue lying around to attract her attention. But the room looked tidy enough and bore no trace of their ill-fated visit.

Matron opened the cupboard. "There are some old shirts and pullovers here that you can have," she said, rummaging through the shelves. "And I rather think there's an old pair of jeans about somewhere."

"Yes, Matron: under those cardboard breast-plates," the boy replied without thinking.

She looked at him curiously. "You've got good eyesight. How do *you* know what's underneath the breast-plates?"

"Well, I just thought, perhaps, there *might* be a pair. It's the sort of place where you could easily find an old pair of jeans, isn't it?" He'd slipped up badly there, Darbishire scolded himself! Nearly given the game away! She must have known he couldn't see from where he was standing.

Matron took down an armful of cast-off garments and carried them across to the table. There wasn't much room to spread them out, for half the table-top was already taken up by clothes in daily use waiting to be mended by the sewing maid. Among them were Temple's socks, Blotwell's torn pullover, Binns' button-less raincoat and, on top of the pile, Mr. Wilkins' old sports jacket which he had brought in that morning for minor repairs.

Matron pushed the everyday clothes to one end of the table and set down her bundle on the other. "There you are, then, Darbishire. Take your pick!"

Darbishire set about his task as though choosing an *ensemble* for a royal garden party, and after some minutes of painstaking indecision on his part, Matron's foot was tapping with impatience.

"Come along, make up your mind for goodness' sake, or we shall be here all night," she complained as he dithered between the choice of a striped pyjama jacket or a coloured shirt. "After all, it's only for a guy! It's going to be burnt, anyway."

"Ah, yes, Matron, but we want him to look stylish." Darbishire's tone was earnest. He was taking his responsibilities seriously. "You see, there's only me here to do the choosing, so I've got some pretty important decisions to make."

He was still ferreting through the junk and making important decisions five minutes later, when Atkinson put his head round the corner and said: "Oh, there you are, Matron! Bromwich is feeling sick in the dispensary. I said I'd tell you."

"I'll come right away," she replied. "It'll be a change from watching old Fashion Plate, here, picking out the latest models." In the doorway she turned and added: "Just take what you want, Darbishire, and leave the rest on the table. I'll put it away afterwards."

"Yes, Matron. Thank you, Matron."

"And whatever you do, don't get the junk mixed up with the mending!"

"No, Matron. Of course not. As though I would!"

Despite his good intentions, the sewing-room table looked like the bargain counter at a rummage sale when Darbishire had finished choosing a trend-setting outfit for the guy. Before leaving, he made an attempt to tidy up, but by now everything was in a muddle and the clothing was no longer in two separate piles.

Still, not to worry, he told himself! Matron would soon have the table looking shipshape when she got back. She was pretty good at that sort of thing!

Well pleased with his efforts, he tucked his chosen bundle under his arm and wandered off downstairs to look for Venables and Temple. He found them in the tuck-box room trying to patch a hole in the guy's left leg where the sacking was rotten and the straw kept coming through.

"Hey, how about these, then!" he sang out, tossing the bundle at them across the room. "Ye very latest men's fashions, as advertised in the newspapers."

Darbishire had made a tasteful selection: a pink shirt, faded blue jeans, an old sports jacket, a panama hat, two left-hand gloves, one large bedroom slipper and one small gym shoe.

The choice was warmly approved by Venables and Temple, who at once began dressing the flabby torso in its ludicrous costume. As the last garment was being coaxed over the straw-filled arms, Temple said: "I say, this is Old Wilkie's jacket. The one he refs football in."

"Well, he won't be reffing football in it any more," said Venables. "Not after today."

"Matron said I could have it," Darbishire assured them. "She said I could take anything except the things to be mended."

Temple nodded. "That's all right, then. It's time old Sir bought himself a new one, anyway."

When the guy was dressed they propped it in a sitting position on the tuck-box rack and stood round it admiring the effect.

Venables said: "Jolly good, isn't it! It even *looks* a bit like Old Wilkie in that jacket. That'll be good for a laugh when the other chaps see it."

Darbishire tilted the panama hat at a more rakish angle and said: "We'll have to buy a mask for him, of course—or make one. That can be a job for Jennings."

"Where is old Jen?" asked Venables. "I thought you two were doing the clobber-choosing together."

Darbishire pulled a face. "We *were*, but he had an accident that nobody's allowed to know about."

Their eyes dilated with curiosity. "What happened? You can tell us, surely," Temple urged. "We're not masters!"

"No, but—" Darbishire paused and considered. Obviously the security arrangements wouldn't apply to present company. "Well, you know the key of the pav? And you know it's still missing?"

"I should think we jolly well do," said Temple. "The Head's been waffling about nothing else at Assembly all this week."

"Yes, well, it's in old Jen's pocket. He—sort of—confiscated it from Old Wilkie when he wasn't about, and it opens the sewing-room as well."

They frowned at him, not understanding. Darbishire wasn't making himself at all clear.

"Go on, then! So what?"

"He had to do some pretty quick thinking when he couldn't wash the paint off. You wouldn't know about that, of course, because you weren't there."

His audience still looked blank, so Darbishire described the disaster in the sewing-room and gave them a brief outline of The Plan of the Secret Haircut.

They listened, agog with excitement.

"Trust Jennings to think out some crafty scheme," Venables said when the tale was told. "And where is he now?"

"Now? At this very particular moment, do you mean?" Darbishire asked. He looked at his watch. It was five-twenty-seven precisely, British Standard Time. "Well, according to his famous, split-second, fail-safe time schedule, Jennings is now, at this very moment, standing at the bus stop in Dunhambury, waiting for the five-thirty bus!"

Darbishire was wrong. Jennings was not, at that moment of time, waiting at the Dunhambury bus stop. Indeed, he was nowhere near the bus stop. He was still skulking behind the showcase in the hairdressing saloon, chafing with frustration and wondering how much longer Mr. Wilkins was going to take having his hair cut.

Seven minutes had ticked by since he had darted for cover, and with every passing second the situation had grown more desperate. Now he was approaching deadline. Unless he was out of the shop in one minute he wouldn't have a hope of catching the bus: if he was missing at tea-time there would be an inquiry and the facts of his escapade would come to light—the unlawful possession of the missing key, the illegal entry into the sewing-room, the outwitting of the duty master, the unauthorised bus journey, the—

Suddenly Jennings stiffened and caught his breath ... From his refuge behind the cupboard he could just see Mr. Wilkins' reflection in the mirror; and as he watched, he saw the assistant removing the barber's cape from his customer's shoulders.

His ordeal was over! Mr. Wilkins was going—but only just in time! He'd allow him a few moments to turn the corner into the car park, he decided, and then he'd run full pelt in the other direction. With any luck he'd be at the bus stop with seconds to spare.

But the next moment his hopes were shattered: the assistant, having shaken out the cape, replaced it around his customer ... Mr. Wilkins was staying on to have his hair shampooed!

Jennings could have wept with disappointment. Numb with dismay, he watched the hairdresser move the chair closer to the wall and saw Mr. Wilkins sit forward and bend his head down over the basin.

Then, as he watched, an idea born of desperation flashed through his mind. If Mr. Wilkins had his head in the basin, he could no longer see what was going on behind him! Now was the moment to escape! Now or never!

With his cap clutched tightly in his hand, Jennings left the safety of his hiding-place and tiptoed along the shop. He wanted to run, but was afraid that the sound of hurrying footsteps might cause Mr. Wilkins to look up.

So he crept forward like a cat on spiked railings, too intent on the perils of his plight to notice Mr. Hales' smile of encouragement or the curious stares of the waiting customers. He drew level with Mr. Wilkins' chair and still his luck was holding. The door was a mere six feet away, and the doorway led to safety.

He went on. He reached the door and was stretching out for the handle when Mr. Wilkins raised his head from the basin and caught sight of the fugitive's reflection in the mirror.

"Ah, Jennings!" he said.

CHAPTER 8

Plan of Campaign

THE BOY JUMPED like a startled rabbit and swung round in dismay. His throat was dry: he could not speak. He stood gaping stupidly, waiting for the obvious questions and the ensuing outburst of anger.

Surprisingly, they never came! Instead, Mr. Wilkins said: "I must say you look a lot tidier now you've had your hair cut, Jennings—less like a thatched roof that the birds had got into. I hardly recognised you." He spoke in friendly, jocular tones with no trace of surprise or indignation.

Jennings was thunderstruck. What on earth had come over Old Wilkie! Why wasn't he demanding explanations and threatening punishments? His astonishment increased as the master went on: "Hang on a few minutes until I'm ready, and I'll run you back to school. You can go and wait in my car if you like. It's round the corner in the car park."

"Yes, sir. Thank you, sir."

In a daze of bewilderment, Jennings tottered out of the shop and made his way to the car park nearby, where Mr. Wilkins' car was standing some distance from the entrance. The doors were unlocked, so he climbed into the passenger seat and sat trying to see some glimmer of sense in the latest turn of events.

But there *was* no glimmer! Whichever way he looked at it, he could find no reason for Mr. Wilkins' attitude. Consider the facts! He'd been caught red-handed, out of bounds, doing something so unusual that any school-master would be bound to demand an explanation.

And Mr. Wilkins had accepted the situation as though it was the most natural thing in the world. Not a single question! Not a word of rebuke! ... It was incredible!

But what was baffling to Jennings was as clear as day to Mr. Wilkins. For only two days before, during staff supper, the headmaster had decided that the boy should go to Dunhambury on the next half-holiday to have his hair cut. So it was no surprise to Mr. Wilkins to find that their visits had coincided.

Jennings stopped racking his brains and looked idly at the instrument panel in front of him. The ignition key was in its socket, attached to a ring from which a number of other keys were hanging.

He leaned forward and looked more closely. Why, of course! Here was the key-ring which so seldom left its owner's possession: the ring from which he had borrowed the pavilion key with the distinctive blob of green paint on its shaft .... Here, too, was his chance to return it with no questions asked!

He glanced round the car park, but there was no sign of Mr. Wilkins. Quickly, he took the borrowed key from his pocket and added it to the bundle hanging from the ignition switch. Then he heaved a sigh of relief. He had the feeling that the wretched thing would have burned a hole in his pocket if he had kept it much longer!

A few minutes later Mr. Wilkins, with hair neatly trimmed, came striding up the line of parked cars.

"All set!" he boomed pleasantly as he sank into the driving seat. "Just as well I spotted you. I doubt whether you'd have caught the five-thirty bus by the time you'd got to the bus stop."

He switched on the ignition and started the engine.

Jennings kept a watchful eye on the driver during the journey. But at no time—not even when they arrived at school—did Mr. Wilkins notice that the missing key was safely back in its usual place.

Venables, Temple and Darbishire were washing their hands for tea when they heard Mr. Wilkins' car draw up on the playground.

Temple was nearest to the window and his gasp of shocked surprise brought the other two hurrying across the room to join him.

"Hey, look! Sir's caught him. He's brought him back in his car."

"Wow! Poor old Jennings! There'll be a gruesome hoo-hah about this when they get indoors," Venables prophesied. "I bet Old Wilkie's in a frantic bate."

Darbishire shook his head sadly. "So much for The Plan of the Secret Haircut! I always knew it wasn't fail-safe, but you can't tell old Jennings anything when once he's made up his mind." He peered into the gathering dusk as master and pupil made their way to the side door. Puzzled, he added: "Old Wilkie doesn't look in a bate, though. I heard him laughing just then."

"Well, of *course* he's laughing," said Temple. "Cackling with fiendish glee at the thought of what he's going to do to his poor wretched victim, squirming on the hook." He made for the door. "Come on, let's find out what happened. I don't want to miss this."

When the boys reached the hall, the returning travellers were coming in through the side door. Mr. Wilkins appeared to be in excellent spirits.

". . . but I don't think there's any real cause for

alarm," he was saying reassuringly. "It's bound to be safe. I'll have a good look for it this evening."

"Thank you, sir," Jennings replied. "Don't go to any trouble, though. It doesn't matter an awful lot."

"Of course it matters! It's my responsibility and I'm determined to find—" Mr. Wilkins broke off at the sight of Darbishire, Venables and Temple gaping stupidly at him from across the hall. "What's the matter with you three? Don't you recognise Jennings when he's had his hair cut?" His loud laugh boomed out. "I agree it's a bit of a shock to see him looking like a civilised human being, but you must agree it's a change for the better."

Then the tea bell rang and Mr. Wilkins strode off to his room, leaving Jennings smirking self-consciously on the doormat. His bewildered colleagues rushed over to him, showering him with questions.

"What went wrong? How did he catch you? What's going to happen? Why isn't he in a bate?"

Jennings faced the barrage with a confident grin. "Don't panic! Operation completed according to plan —well, not *quite*, but everything's under control."

"Yes, but—"

"No time to explain! Tea bell's gone and I'm hungry. I'll tell you later." Jennings tossed his cap at the nearest peg and hurried off towards the dining-hall. His friends followed, seething with curiosity.

"But what was Sir waffling about when he said there was no cause for alarm?" Venables demanded, grabbing Jennings by the shoulders to slow him down.

"Oh, that! Well, that was nothing to do with ye secret operation," Jennings replied, shrugging himself free. "It was just that I gave him my watch to look after during football one day and he is afraid he can't remember where he's put it."

"Is that all!" Venables was disappointed. "Just like Old Wilkie, of course. The man's a scatterbrain— losing your watch, losing the key of the pav. He'll be losing his head soon if he doesn't screw it on."

"Yes, I dare say." Jennings smiled as though savouring some private joke. "You needn't worry about the pav key, though. I've got a feeling that it'll turn up again, one of these fine days."

It was not until they were going to bed that evening that the boys in Dormitory 4 had a chance to hear the true story of the afternoon's activities. They listened with attention, weighed the good luck against the bad, and gave Jennings full marks for his handling of a difficult situation. Trust Jennings! was their verdict. He'd get away with it if anyone could!

But what nobody could understand was Mr. Wilkins' extraordinary behaviour when faced with a clear breach of school rules. Why he hadn't pounced on the culprit and brought him to justice must rank as one of the most baffling mysteries of modern times.

Venables sat up in bed and said: "Mind you, I agree old Jennings did pretty well, all things considered. But if it had been me, I bet I could have got past Old Wilkie without even being spotted."

"How?" Atkinson demanded.

"Well, he'd got this Guy Fawkes mask in his pocket, hadn't he! Okay, then, he could have put it on and marched out of the shop and Old Wilkie wouldn't have recognised him. Quite a crafty plan, actually."

Jennings, the master-planner, hooted with derision. "Honestly, Venables, you need your brains tested. I've heard some pretty ropey wheezes in my time, but that one takes the parchment diploma." From his bedside stool he picked up the mask which he had brought up to the dormitory for his friends' inspection. "Supposing I'd gone waltzing past him in my school tie, school socks and school pullover, with my cap in my hand and this thing on my face!"

By way of demonstration, he donned the grotesque plastic face, jumped out of bed and teetered down the dormitory, waving his arms in ludicrous gestures. When he reached Venables' bed he stopped and said: "I suppose you think Old Wilkie would have said to himself, 'Ah! here comes a boy from Linbury Court School with a nose like a cricket ball and a walrus moustache. It's funny I haven't noticed him before. Must be a new boy!' "

Having made his point, Jennings danced back along the dormitory and skidded to a halt beside his bed as Mr. Carter came into the room to call silence.

"An unnerving spectacle!" the master observed, flinching in mock terror. "It's quite destroyed my appetite for supper."

Jennings took off the mask and grinned. "Did you recognise me, sir? Would you have known who it was if I'd kept it on?"

Mr. Carter's features remained grave. "Surely you know, Jennings, that all schoolmasters have eyes like photo-electric burglar alarms. They can penetrate even the most baffling of disguises!"

Temple, sleeping next to Venables, leaned across the gangway between the beds and whispered: "There you are! That proves it. So much for your crafty old plan!"

Mr. Carter put out the dormitory light and went down to the staff room, where several of the masters had foregathered for supper. The head-master was looking carefully through a desk diary, engrossed in checking future arrangements.

"Ah, there you are, Carter! A word with you about Bonfire Night," he began. "I've sent out invitations to a number of local people, as you suggested, and I also let them know that I've given permission for one or two boys to take a collection for charity after the fireworks are over."

"Splendid," Mr. Carter agreed. "It was mainly Form 3's idea in the first place, you know. Jennings and his friends are hoping to raise a worthwhile sum for famine relief."

"I'm glad to hear that Jennings is at last—" Mr. Pemberton-Oakes broke off, and a flicker of annoyance passed over his features. "Tut! What a nuisance! Speaking of Jennings reminds me that I meant to send him to have his hair cut this afternoon, and I forgot all about it."

Mr. Wilkins looked up from the evening paper. "You forgot, H.M.? But surely you must have told him. I met him in the hairdresser's in Dunhambury and gave him a lift back."

"Really! That's very odd! Did you ask who had told him to go?"

"It never occurred to me. I assumed he was there on your instructions."

"No, I never gave the matter another thought until this moment. So why on earth—!" Suddenly the head-master's puzzled frown gave place to a look of comprehension. "Ah, yes, of course, it must have been Matron. She was there when we were discussing it during supper the other evening. I'm glad she remembered to tell him."

As it happened, Matron was not present to disclaim responsibility, and Mr. Pemberton-Oakes went on to talk of other matters. . . . And upstairs in Dormitory 4 Jennings settled down to sleep, unaware that he had just had another lucky escape from impending disaster.

On certain half-holidays the Linbury boys were allowed to go to the village after football to buy sweets or anything else of which they were in need. It was this custom which Jennings and his friends proposed to bend to their own purpose, by applying for leave in a lawful manner but using the occasion to display their guy in the village street and wave collecting boxes under the noses of the passers-by.

Village leave was a privilege which could be forfeited as a punishment for misbehaviour or unsatisfactory progress in class. But on the first Saturday in November the five members of the Special Action Sub-committee of the Form 3 Fireworks Fund were free from all forms of detention when they assembled on the front steps at four o'clock to give in their names to the master on duty.

"Jennings, Darbishire, Atkinson, Venables, Temple," Mr. Carter said, jotting down their names on his list. "Report back by five-thirty, and don't be late."

"Yes, sir . . . No, sir!"

They set off walking sedately down the drive, but once out of sight of the school building they veered off to the right, skirted the playing-fields and made for the tool-shed behind the kitchen garden.

"We're going out by the back gate," Darbishire told Atkinson, who had been absent during Jennings' briefing in the tuck-box room. "If we go over the field-path we're not likely to meet anybody on the way."

"Yes, but where's the guy?" the Public Relations Officer wanted to know. "I thought we were taking him with us."

"So we are. He's in the tool-shed. Temple and Venables smuggled him down there yesterday evening and hid him under the sacks. And there's a sort of trolley thing in there that Temple thinks will be just the job to cart him around on."

They reached the tool-shed without incident, removed the guy from under the potato sacks and tied it to a broken dustbin trolley which was to serve as its chariot. With the plastic mask in place, the panama hat askew, and Mr. Wilkins' sports jacket strained at the seams around the portly torso, there was no doubt in the minds of the Action Sub-committee that the effigy was a work of considerable artistic merit.

"Budge out of the way! Bags I wheel him," said Jennings, trundling the trolley out through the tool-shed door. "And all keep a look-out for masters. I don't suppose we'll meet anybody who matters, but you never know."

Nobody was about as the procession went down the muddy track to the back gate. Avoiding the road, they branched off over the footpath across Arrowsmith's farm heading towards the village.

The path was pitted with the wheel ruts of Farmer Arrowsmith's tractors; and after a few hundred yards one of the wheels dropped off the trolley.

Jennings threw it in the ditch and said: "We haven't time to mend it. I'll balance the trolley on one wheel, while you chaps hold the other side up."

Progress was slow and far from easy, but at last they reached Linbury and propelled their ill-balanced vehicle along the village street. They stopped a short distance away from the General Stores and Post Office, where a footpath leading to a row of cottages ran off at right angles to the main road.

"This is the drill! I've got it all worked out, copyright reserved," Jennings announced when the trolley was safely propped against the wall of a nearby front garden. "Darbi, Atki and I will do the collecting, and Temple and Ven are the security guards at each end of the street." He turned to the sentries. "Your job is to stand where you can see round the bend and wave your handkerchief if you see a master's car coming along. That'll give the rest of us time to hide our collecting boxes and stroll up to the Stores as though we're just going in to buy sweets."

"And what about the guy?" asked Atkinson.

"We leave him where he is. Nobody will know he's anything to do with us if we don't take any notice of him. And then, when the master's gone sailing past, we can come out of the shop and go on collecting."

"Suppose he sees us waving?" Venables queried.

"Well, why not! We're on village leave, aren't we! There's no rule about not giving a master a friendly wave as he drives by."

From his raincoat pockets Darbishire produced two cylindrical cocoa tins with slits pierced in the lids. Sticky labels round the circumference bore the words *Support Famine Relief* boldly inscribed with a felt pen.

"Here's one for you, Atki. Jennings has got his own," Darbishire said, handing over one of the tins. "I've put two pence in so that we can start off with a good rattle, but you'll have to pay it back before we count the takings."

The leader took up his position on the pavement beside the guy. "Right! Action Stations!" he commanded.

The self-appointed ginger-group moved away to their posts . . . *The Secret Fund Raising Expedition* © *Copyright by J. C. T. Jennings* was under way!

CHAPTER 9

Penny for the Guy

IT WOULD BE stretching the facts to describe the village
of Linbury, tucked away in a fold of the South
Downs, as a busy centre of rural life.

Despite the attractions of its medieval church, its
petrol-filling station and its three small shops, most of
the inhabitants prefer to catch the bus into Dunhambury on Saturday afternoons rather than do their
shopping or pursue their leisure on their native heath.

Thus it was that few people were about to admire
the effigy on the dustbin trolley; and fewer still were
willing to support a worthy cause with a contribution
in cash. After rattling their cocoa tins outside the
General Stores and Post Office for twenty minutes,
Darbishire had collected three pence and a free
coupon for a cake of soap, Atkinson had a Belgian
franc and four trading stamps, and Jennings had
nothing at all.

The only people who showed interest in the venture
were other Linbury boys on village leave; but they,
also, had no money to spare and nothing to give but
encouragement.

"How's it going?" Bromwich and Martin-Jones
asked as they passed the guy on their way back to
school. They were carrying boxes of fireworks specially
ordered by the Form 3 Fireworks Fund and supplied
by the General Stores.

"Trade's a bit slack at the moment," Jennings admitted. "I'm not worried, though. Things are bound to brighten up a bit soon."

As though in answer to his prophecy, little Miss Thorpe of Oaktree Cottage came cycling down the road—and things brightened up at once!

Miss Thorpe was a sharp-featured, middle-aged spinster of tireless energy who played an active part in organising the village social life. She was neat and dainty—almost birdlike—in appearance: the fluttering of her gestures and the chirruping of her speech gave one the impression of a busy blue-tit prospecting for peanuts. The boys knew her well, for she was a frequent visitor at the school, and on several occasions they had been involved in her parish activities.

As she dismounted outside the Stores, Darbishire advanced to meet her, jingling his collecting tin. "Good afternoon, Miss Thorpe! That's our Guy Fawkes over there," he said, smiling politely. "I wonder whether you'd care to contribute to our—"

He got no further. For instead of returning his greeting with her usual friendly smile, Miss Thorpe glared at him like a kestrel poised to pounce on a fieldmouse.

"Disgraceful! You ought to be ashamed of yourselves! The very idea!" Her voice, which was usually the trill of a thrush on a spring morning, now shrilled out like a myna bird protesting at the quality of the food in its feeding-dish.

Darbishire was flabbergasted. "I beg your pardon?" he queried.

"Penny for the guy, indeed!" She flung out a hand towards the effigy on the trolley. "I think it's scandalous. How you have the audacity to stand there cadging coppers from the public merely to spend on sweets and fireworks for your own selfish pleasure!"

Jennings hurried forward to explain. "Oh, but Miss Thorpe, you don't understand. We're only—"

"I understand perfectly. Begging—that's all it is! Using November the fifth as an excuse to badger people into parting with their hard-earned money. I shall tell Mr. Pemberton-Oakes exactly what I think of your behaviour. I am surprised that he allows this sort of thing to take place in his school."

"But Miss Thorpe, that's not fair! We're not collecting for ourselves."

But she was in full spate and didn't even hear the interruption.

"And to think that while you well-fed, well-clothed boys are begging in the streets, deprived children in other parts of the world are in dire need. Surely it's your duty to spare a thought for those less fortunate than yourselves."

Miss Thorpe paused for breath and Jennings jumped in quickly. "That's exactly what we *are* doing," he insisted. "We're not collecting for ourselves. We're raising money for famine relief. Read what it says on the collecting tin!"

She read the label; and at once her expression changed. No longer the predatory kestrel, she now looked like a pathetic starling trapped under a strawberry net.

"Oh, dear! I *am* so sorry. I didn't know; I didn't realise," she apologised. "If it is for charity that's *quite* different. I approve wholeheartedly. Indeed I do!"

"It's part of our project to help Mr. Carter's fund," Jennings explained. "And we're going to take a collection on Bonfire Night as well."

"Yes, yes, I shall be there. I've already accepted Mr.

Oakes' invitation," Miss Thorpe assured him. "Do forgive me for jumping to the wrong conclusion. We get so many children asking for pennies for the guy that I thought it was time to take a firm stand!" She fumbled in her purse and produced twenty pence. "But if it's for a really good cause, that's a different kettle of fish, isn't it!"

The coins tinkled down into the cocoa tin and Miss Thorpe, beaming with goodwill, propped her bicycle against the kerb and disappeared into the Stores.

"Phew!" Jennings mopped his brow and sagged at the knees in mock relief. "That was a nasty moment, wasn't it!"

Darbishire nodded. "Decent of her, though. Especially if she coughs up another contribution after the fireworks."

Atkinson had retired to a safe distance at the first shrill note of Miss Thorpe's indignation. Now he wandered back again bored and disappointed with the meagre takings in his tin. "We'll have to pack up pretty soon if we've got to get the old guy back in his shed by half-past five."

He glanced along the street in the Dunhambury direction and gave Jennings a violent nudge in the ribs. "Hey, look! Temple's waving!" he cried.

Temple was indeed waving—and had been for some seconds. He was now jumping about in a state of agitation, furious with the collectors for not keeping a proper look-out for his signals.

The cause of his alarm was Mr. Wilkins' car which had now passed the sentry and was approaching at a careful twenty-nine miles per hour.

Acting upon orders, the collectors quickly hid their tins beneath their raincoats and sauntered towards the

Stores as though on an innocent shopping expedition for their weekly sweet ration . . . But they had not sauntered ten yards when their ruse was thrown into sudden confusion. Instead of driving straight through the village, as they had expected, Mr. Wilkins' car was slowing down and was obviously going to stop at the General Stores.

Jennings thought fast. Miss Thorpe was already inside the shop: in a matter of moments Mr. Wilkins would be there too. It would be fatal for the boys to follow; for if the adults should start talking together the conspirators would be caught in the cross-fire of their conversation. Miss Thorpe would be certain to mention the guy as soon as the boys came in.

Grabbing his fellow-collectors by the arm, Jennings hissed: "Change of plan! Quick, follow me!"

He spun round and darted off down the narrow lane leading away from the main road towards the cottages. Darbishire and Atkinson, alarmed and bewildered, followed hard behind their leader until, twenty yards along the lane, he stopped in the shelter of a quick-thorn hedge.

"What's the idea?" Atkinson demanded breathlessly.

"We're better off down here, with Sir nattering to Miss Thorpe in the Stores," Jennings explained. "We'd be crazy to go in too."

"Do you think she'll tell him?"

Jennings shrugged. "We'll have to risk that. She probably thinks we've got permission. But if Old Wilkie's in a hurry and we're not there to answer questions, we may get away with it."

This was the best they could hope for!

"What do we do next?" Darbishire wanted to know.

"Wait till Sir's driven off," Jennings decided. "As

soon as we see him drive away, it'll be safe to go back."

At times of crisis Darbishire always kept his fingers crossed and allowed himself three wishes to stave off disaster. He did so now!

"Please let Miss Thorpe keep her mouth shut," he wished. "Please let Sir be in a hurry. Please let him drive off before I count fifty."

Darbishire's first two wishes came true. Miss Thorpe was so busy chatting to the assistant at the provisions' counter that she didn't even notice Mr. Wilkins come into the shop. And Mr. Wilkins, having little time to spare, bought his tin of tobacco and strode out of the Stores with no more than a polite "Good afternoon, Miss Thorpe," as he made for the door.

And, indeed, Darbishire's third wish might also have been granted but for one important factor that Jennings had overlooked. Guys were a common sight on the Saturday preceding the fifth of November, and normally Mr. Wilkins would not have looked twice at the seasonal effigy in the village street. . . . But as he was getting into his car he noticed that the guy was wearing a sports jacket of a familiar style and colour.

Mr. Wilkins looked again. It couldn't really be *his* jacket, he reasoned—that was impossible! And yet it looked identical, even to the well-worn leather patches on the elbows. Puzzled, he got out of the car and went up to the guy to investigate.

At once his eyebrows rose in surprise. There was no doubt about it! It was his jacket which he had assumed was still in the sewing-room awaiting minor repairs. What on earth was it doing swathed round this shapeless bundle of straw and sacking outside the Linbury General Stores and Post Office!

Baffled, the master looked up and down the road for

some clue to the mystery, but the security guards had bolted for cover and there was no one in sight. Then he glanced down the lane leading to the cottages and was just in time to see a human head pop back into the shelter of the quick-thorn hedge.

Mr. Wilkins recognised the head. It belonged to the wishful Darbishire who, having counted up to forty-seven, was risking a quick glance at the main road in the hope of seeing the master's car go by before he had got up to fifty.

In a voice like a loud-hailer, Mr. Wilkins boomed: "Darbishire! Come here, at once!"

Darbishire emerged, followed by Jennings and Atkinson, who saw no further reason for hiding now that the game was up.

"What in the name of reason do you boys think you're playing at?" the master stormed as the conspirators came out of the lane and stood before him looking sheepish. "Are you responsible for this horrible object on the trolley?"

"It's our guy, sir," Jennings explained. "But it's all right, sir. We got permission to make one for Bonfire Night."

"Maybe you did! But you didn't get permission to trundle the wretched thing all round the village, did you!"

"Well, not exactly, sir. But we thought it would be all right because we're helping Mr. Carter collect money for famine relief, you see, and Matron gave us these old clothes to dress him up in and—"

"*Matron* did!" Mr. Wilkins was thunderstruck. "Matron gave you my perfectly good sports jacket to throw on the bonfire?"

"She didn't actually *give* it to us, sir," Darbishire

conceded. "But she said we could help ourselves to the worn-out old stuff in the sewing-room that wasn't wanted again."

"But it *is* wanted again! I didn't leave it there because I'd finished with it. I left it there to be mended."

"Oh! Oh, I see. Sorry, sir, I didn't realise," Darbishire mumbled. Now he came to think of it, he *had* made rather a muddle of the garments on the sewing-room table. Still, it was a pure accident: if the tatty old jacket had got into the wrong pile, it wasn't fair to blame the chap who'd done the sorting out. It was surely up to Mr. Wilkins to look after his own belongings!

But Mr. Wilkins didn't seem to think so. "It's disgraceful," he fumed. "Irresponsible behaviour and wanton disregard for other people's property! I've a good mind to ask the headmaster to cancel the fireworks and bonfire next Tuesday. And furthermore, I shall—"

"Cancel the bonfire! Oh, but Mr. Wilkins, that would be unthinkable! It's such a wonderful opportunity for the boys to help in a worthy cause."

The interruption came from behind him and, turning, Mr. Wilkins saw Miss Thorpe standing at his elbow looking at him with the dismayed expression of a blackbird eyeing a fast-burrowing earthworm. "I think it's splendid that these boys are willing to devote their leisure time to making a guy and collecting funds for their less fortunate brothers and sisters."

Politely, Mr. Wilkins said: "I don't think you quite understand, Miss Thorpe. I've no objection to their making a guy if they want to. What I'm complaining about is their audacity in purloining my clothes to dress it up in."

She gave him a winning smile. "Ah, well! Boys will be boys! And I'm sure you won't spoil the fun, considering what good work these lads are doing." She moved away to her bicycle and hung her shopping bag on the handlebars. "We are all *so* looking forward to the fireworks on Tuesday, so mind you boys have your collecting boxes at the ready," she chirruped as she mounted her machine. "I think it's splendid to see masters and boys all working together in a common cause. Don't you agree, Mr. Wilkins?"

Mr. Wilkins frowned with annoyance as the frail cyclist pedalled away down the street. He had intended to deal severely with the boys and had been on the point of imposing a punishment when Miss Thorpe had intervened . . . But now she had taken the wind out of his sails. All this talk of good works and worthy causes implied that he—L. P. Wilkins, Esq.—would be acting in a churlish manner if he failed to pull his weight in the communal effort. She was, in fact, accusing him of being more concerned to save his shabby old coat than to help the cause of famine relief.

This was plainly absurd! The boys deserved to be punished and yet—and yet—! Mr. Wilkins couldn't make up his mind. Tersely, he said: "Go back to school at once, you boys, and take that ridiculous guy with you."

Then he strode back to his car and drove off, staring straight ahead with a scowl of disapproval.

Matron was talking to Mr. Carter in the entrance hall when Mr. Wilkins arrived back at school. His temper was still ruffled from his encounter in the village and he looked at Matron with a resentful frown. She was partly to blame for his discomfiture, he thought, and he felt justified in making a complaint.

"I say, Matron, it really is too bad," he said reproachfully. "I took my sports jacket along to the sewing-room to have it *mended*. I certainly didn't expect you to give it to Form 3 for their guy."

She looked surprised. "But I didn't," she said.

"No? Well, they've got it, anyway. I've just found Jennings and his cronies parading their wretched effigy round the village dressed up in *my* clothing, if you please!"

Matron laughed. "Trust Jennings! I expect it got mixed up with the cast-offs. Sorry about that." She paused. "You'll let them keep it, won't you?"

"Let them *keep* it!" Mr. Wilkins was outraged. "I should jolly well think *not*. I use that jacket every time I take football practice."

She shrugged. "Just as you like. But it's a very *old* jacket, Mr. Wilkins. It's hardly worth mending, really."

"I agree," Mr. Carter chimed in. "High time you bought yourself a new one, Wilkins. Besides, think of all the money the boys are hoping to raise at the bonfire. Surely you wouldn't begrudge them that ancient old relic! I should have thought you'd be only too pleased to make a slight sacrifice for the sake of a worthy cause."

Mr. Wilkins was taken aback. Instead of sharing his indignation they were siding with the boys and closing ranks against him. All of them, Miss Thorpe, Matron—even Carter! . . . H'm! What should he do? It *was* a worthy cause, admittedly, but all the same—!

As he pondered the matter, Mr. Wilkins was idly toying with the key-ring which he had removed from his ignition switch a few minutes earlier. Suddenly he became aware that his colleague was looking at him in puzzled wonder.

"Correct me if I'm wrong," Mr. Carter said gently. "But isn't that key with the green blob on it the one that everybody has been searching for?"

Mr. Wilkins glanced down, his jaw dropped through an angle of forty-five degrees, and he stared at the metal object he was holding as though expecting its jagged teeth to bite his finger.

"Good heavens! The key of the pavilion!" he gasped.

"Exactly," Mr. Carter confirmed. "It would have saved a great deal of trouble if you had produced it ten days ago."

"But I didn't know where it was! I've only just found it. How did it get there?"

"I imagine you must have put it back in a fit of absentmindedness."

"I did no such thing!"

"Then somebody else must have replaced it in your absence."

"That's impossible! Quite out of the question," Mr. Wilkins maintained. "I give you my word that this key-ring hasn't left my possession since the day of the Bracebridge match. I've always carried it about with me in my trouser pocket—except when I'm driving the car."

"Well, if *you* didn't put it back and no one else did either—" Mr. Carter left the sentence unfinished, and Mr. Wilkins became aware that both his colleagues were regarding him with anxious concern. They were giving him the sort of look which suggested that these obvious delusions and signs of mental strain were probably the result of teaching Form 3 for fourteen periods a week.

Just then the side door to the playground swung open and Jennings came in carrying Mr. Wilkins' jacket over his arm.

"Please, sir, here's your coat, sir," he said as he crossed the hall. "We're sorry we—sort of—borrowed it by mistake."

"Are you indeed!"

"Yes, sir. But we talked it over on the way back from the village and we've taken it off the guy because you seemed so—er—so upset about it." He stood holding out the jacket and shifting his feet awkwardly.

Mr. Wilkins hesitated for a moment and then waved the garment aside with a dramatic sweep of the arm. "Keep it! Take it away! Put it back on the guy," he commanded in ringing tones.

"Oh, but sir, we thought—"

"I've changed my mind. I shall be delighted to watch it go up in flames on the bonfire." Mr. Wilkins gave a little self-conscious laugh. "You surely don't imagine I'm the sort of person who would hamper a worthy cause for the sake of a shabby old sports coat!"

"No, sir. Of course not, sir. Thank you very much, sir. Thank you very much indeed."

The boy turned to go, the jacket clasped in his arms. But halfway across the hall a thought struck him and he swung round and said: "Oh, by the way, sir, have you found my watch yet, by any chance?"

"Not yet, I'm afraid, Jennings." Mr. Wilkins gave him a reassuring smile. "Don't worry, though. It can't be far away. It's sure to be about somewhere."

Mr. Carter flashed Matron a knowing look. "Like the key of the pavilion!" he said in ominous tones.

CHAPTER 10

Bonfire Night

THERE WAS NO football practice on Monday and Tuesday. Instead, the whole school spent their games periods in gathering brushwood and branches and building the traditional bonfire on the patch of rough ground beyond the playing-fields.

Form 3, in particular, took an active part in the preparations. Pettigrew and Marshall collected the contents of every waste-paper basket in the school to provide kindling for the fire in its early stages. Atkinson (Public Relations Officer to G. Fawkes, Esq., deceased) improvised more collecting boxes labelled *Support Famine Relief*. Bromwich and Martin-Jones helped Mr. Carter to arrange a programme for the fireworks and construct launching-sites for the rockets; and Venables and Temple made sure that the guy would be looking his best for the ritual burning by valeting his costume with a stiff clothes brush.

Jennings and Darbishire spent their free time on Monday in scavenging for timber. Mr. Hind was in charge of stacking the wood on the pile and shaping it into a tidy pyramid. He stood on the top of a tall step-ladder puffing at his cherrywood pipe and encouraging the scavengers in their search for combustible material.

"We haven't got nearly enough yet for a really good blaze," he told Jennings and Darbishire when they appeared at the foot of his ladder bearing useless handfuls of twigs and dead leaves. "Go away and look for some more."

They had already made three expeditions in the previous ten minutes and were growing disheartened.

"There doesn't seem to be any more decent stuff lying about, sir—well, not the sort we can carry by ourselves," Jennings pointed out. "Form 5 have bagged the Head's trailer for the big logs and things, and they won't let us share it."

"You'd better try farther afield, then," the master advised. "Go and see if there's anything stacked by the incinerator in the Head's garden. He's usually got some burnable rubbish at this time of the year and we could save him the trouble of setting light to it."

The boys set off on their errand, and on the way they met Binns and Blotwell, the youngest boys in the school, bowling two worn car tyres over the football pitches at full speed.

"Old Wilkie's cast-offs. He said we could have them for the bonfire," Binns explained when the makeshift hoops had come to rest between the goal-posts. "They'll go up like a bomb and give off lethal, poisonous fumes."

"We've got a crafty scheme plotted out," Blotwell said, contorting his face to denote low cunning. "You see, with any luck all the chaps standing on the windy side of the fire will be overcome by the fumes, so we'll be able to have their bangers and spuds at the barbecue." He cackled with hideous, maniacal laughter. "There's nothing like a good pong of blazing rubber to take the edge off your appetite!"

Jennings and Darbishire exchanged superior glances. "Typical of their tiny minds," Jennings said sadly. "You can't really expect titchy little Form One chaps to think of other people like ordinary human beings."

Darbishire smiled with mock indulgence. "Give them a chance! By the time they grow up into Form Three-ers they may be almost civilised. They say education works wonders—even in hopeless cases."

Unable to think of a face-saving answer, the youngest boys retrieved their tyres and set off on another bowling race. "Don't listen to them! Everyone knows all Form 3 are mad," Blotwell observed as they propelled their rubber hoops towards the bonfire site. "And anyway, I'm still going to stand on the un-windy side of the smoke and hope for the best, whatever they say."

The headmaster's garden was normally out of bounds to the boys, but Mr. Hind's instructions clearly implied permission to go in. So Jennings led the way through the gate and ran along the broad gravel path with Darbishire at his heels.

The incinerator was in a corner of the garden screened from view by an enclosure of wattle hurdles. At first glance there appeared to be no dead shrubs or similar rubbish awaiting incineration, and the boys were about to abandon their quest when Jennings noticed a heap of uprooted young poplar trees lying on the ground not far from the compost heap.

"How about these, then!" he exclaimed. "They'll burn all right."

Darbishire looked doubtful. "How do you know they're not wanted?"

"Of course they're not wanted. He wouldn't have dug them up and chucked them out if they were any good." Jennings pointed to a row of poplars which served as a windbreak some distance away. "That's where they've come from, look! Any fool knows you have to thin these things out every so often and that's what the Head's been doing. This other lot are the ones he wants to get rid of."

It seemed a reasonable assumption. "Righto, then! Take them along to Mr. Hind, shall we!" Darbishire agreed.

It would take several journeys and a great deal of time to transport the poplars by hand, Jennings decided. An easier way would be to use the headmaster's car-trailer if he could persuade the log-collecting fifth-formers to part with it for ten minutes or so. "You'd better come with me, Darbi," he said. "I don't know whether I can manage the trailer on my own."

Together they ran back to the playing-field, where the first thing they saw was Mr. Pemberton-Oakes' trailer parked outside the pavilion. The Form 5 lumber-jacks, having finished their task, had apparently abandoned the vehicle and gone indoors to get ready for tea.

It was a lightweight trailer and the two boys were able to move it without difficulty where the ground was level. With Jennings on the shaft and Darbishire at the rear, they towed it across to the garden and along the path to the compost heap.

Darbishire said: "We'd better get a move on: it's nearly time for tea."

"It shouldn't take long. We can manage them all in one load," Jennings told him.

There were about thirty young poplar trees in the heap and the trailer was piled high by the time they had put them all aboard. Jennings took his place at the shaft and said: "Heave-ho, then, Darbi! This lot ought to please Mr. Hind. Lucky we found them."

The trailer was not so easy to control now that it was laden, but when the boys had towed it as far as the playing-field they met Martin-Jones and Bromwich returning from the rocket launching-site and pressed them into service.

It was beginning to grow dark by now and there was no sign of Mr. Hind and his ladder when they reached the bonfire. So the four boys unloaded the trailer at the edge of the pyre and stacked their offering on the pyramid as best they could. As they tossed the last of the poplars into the brushwood, they could hear the tea bell sounding in the distance.

"That's it, then!" Jennings said with satisfaction, wiping his muddy hands on his anorak. "I don't know about you lot, but I reckon I deserve a medal for all the work I've done this afternoon."

There was no medal for Jennings! . . . Having spent their free time on Monday afternoon in building the bonfire, the school spent morning break on Tuesday in taking it down again.

The trouble started after breakfast when Mr. Pemberton-Oakes went into his garden to inspect the batch of young poplar trees which had been delivered the previous day. To his surprise, there was no sign of them, despite the fact that he himself had seen the nurseryman carrying them in through the garden gate the morning before.

Where on earth had the man hidden them? . . . And then, passing the compost heap, the headmaster noticed divots of mud on the path and tracks on the damp earth where a wheel of the trailer had run wide of the gravel path.

Mr. Pemberton-Oakes followed the wheel-tracks, and once beyond the gate he could see faint tyre marks on the grass and traces of mud and broken twigs leading away towards the newly-erected bonfire.

Five minutes later he found his poplars: and ten minutes after that he came striding into morning assembly looking extremely angry.

"Stand up the boys who went into my garden yesterday afternoon!"

The two culprits rose to their feet. Jennings was puzzled. Was it because they had used the trailer without first asking permission, he wondered?

"Who told you to remove those young trees and throw them on the bonfire?" the headmaster demanded.

So that was it!

"Nobody, sir. We didn't think they were wanted," Jennings faltered. In the hushed assembly hall his voice sounded reedy and unnatural. "We were looking for dead shrubs and things and we thought they'd been dug up and thrown away."

Mr. Pemberton-Oakes, a keen gardener, was shocked by such ignorance.

"Dug up? . . . Thrown away?" he echoed. "Good heavens, boy, they were new trees. They hadn't even been planted, let alone dug up."

"Sorry, sir."

"Sorry! So I should think. Do you realise that you young vandals have thrown away thirty pounds' worth of carefully chosen saplings—a whole avenue of expensive trees. I shall cancel the bonfire this evening . . ." He paused, and there was a gasp of dismay from the lower forms in the front rows . . . "unless every one of those trees is returned to my garden in good condition before the celebrations begin."

The lower forms breathed again. Binns nudged Blotwell and they exchanged knowing winks. It was going to be all right, after all!

Midway down the hall, the culprits subsided in their seats, and Mr. Pemberton-Oakes, tight-lipped with annoyance, went on to the next item of the morning's agenda.

When assembly was over and the masters were leaving the hall, Mr. Wilkins said to his colleague: "I say, Carter, I was surprised at the Head getting so upset just because a couple of boys accidentally walked off with a few spindly saplings. You'd think he'd be only too pleased to make a slight sacrifice for the sake of a worthy cause."

Mr. Carter gave him a look, and passed on!

It took the whole of morning break and most of the afternoon's game period to remove the poplars and re-shape the bonfire. The young trees were so mixed up with the branches and brushwood that, in the end, Mr. Hind decided that the only thing to be done was to demolish the pyre completely and build it up again from scratch.

Needless to say, Jennings and Darbishire were not popular with their fellows, but they managed to restore their reputation by working harder than any-one else: and when the tea bell rang at six o'clock, the bonfire was ready and the poplars were safely back in the headmaster's garden.

The guests arrived at half-past six and were enter-tained in Mr. Pemberton-Oakes' drawing-room while they waited for the celebrations to start.

Miss Thorpe was there with a purse full of change in her handbag, and Dr. Furnival, the school medical officer. Also present were General Merridew, Linbury's most distinguished Old Boy, the Arrowsmiths from the farm, Dr. Hipkin (known to Jennings and his friends

as the Scientific Frogman*), the vicar of Linbury, and
several more.

Robinson, the school cleaner, had made some dozens
of flares consisting of thick felt pads nailed to a stick
and soaked in paraffin. And at seven o'clock, when the
guests appeared at the front door, the boys lighted their
flares, formed a line, and led the way to the bonfire.

At the tail of the torchlight procession came G.
Fawkes, Esq. (deceased), carried shoulder-high by the
self-appointed ginger-group of the Form 3 Fireworks
Fund.

The guy's stylish costume was the subject of some
comment.

"I wonder where the lads unearthed that dreadful
old sports jacket," General Merridew remarked loudly
as the effigy was borne past. "I can't imagine anybody
actually *wearing* a thing like that." He laughed heartily.
"It looks like something left over from a scarecrows'
jumble sale."

Mr. Wilkins, standing beside him in the darkness,
blew his nose to cover his embarrassment. He had been
very fond of that jacket!

When the tail of the procession reached the unlit
bonfire, the bearers halted and waited for Mr. Hind to
erect his step-ladder to carry the guy aloft. As they
stood there, Jennings shifted his grip on the guy's body
and felt his fingers press against something round and
flat inside the lining of his jacket.

At first he thought it was a coin and he thrust his
hand into the side pocket hoping to retrieve it. But it
was too thick for a coin, and though he could still feel
it he couldn't free it from the folds of the material.
It must have slipped through a hole and be trapped in

*See *Take Jennings for Instance*

the lining. His fingers sought out the hole and tore it wider apart. Then he groped below the lining into the hem of the garment and drew out a wrist-watch attached to its strap.

For a moment he stared at it with unbelieving eyes in the flickering light of the flares. Then he gave a great shout of recognition.

"Wow! Look what I've found—my watch!"

The other members of the guy's bodyguard looked at him in surprise.

"Your watch! Don't be crazy," said Temple. "It must be Old Wilkie's."

"It's mine, I tell you! He was wearing this coat when I gave it to him during football. No wonder he couldn't find it, underneath the lining."

The boy wound it up, shook it, and made sure that it was ticking. As he was strapping it on to his wrist, Mr. Wilkins and Mr. Carter came along to help Mr. Hind with his ladder.

"Sir! Sir! I've found my watch, sir," Jennings cried excitedly. "Inside your old jacket, sir."

Mr. Wilkins was delighted. "So that's where it got to! I had a feeling it would turn up sooner or later—and it did!"

"Only just in time. Another minute and it would have been on the bonfire," Mr. Carter pointed out.

Jennings grinned. "Lucky old me! And good old Mr. Wilkins! If you hadn't given us your coat for the guy, sir, my watch would have stayed sewn up in your lining for ever and ever and ever!"

By now the ladder was in place, and Mr. Hind took the guy and climbed up and secured it to the topmost branch of the pyre. When he had come down again and retrieved his flare from Mr. Carter, Blotwell rushed forward and said: "Sir, please, sir, may I light the bonfire for you, sir? I've got a box of coloured matches."

Mr. Hind shook his head. "Sorry, Blotwell, but I think I'd make a better job of it than you. You see—" He paused and held his flaming torch aloft. "I have a flair for this sort of thing."

Mr. Carter groaned at the pun, and Blotwell said: "Oh, sir, was that a joke, sir?"

"Guilty!" Mr. Hind confessed. "It comes of teaching Art to Form 1. After a while you find yourself indulging in their very special brand of humour."

So saying, he thrust his flare into an oil-soaked bundle of straw, and the flames leaped upwards.

The evening was a great success—better, even, than usual, the boys decided. It was as though this year in particular the bonfire seemed bigger, the guy funnier, the fireworks brighter, the explosions louder.

Never before had the barbecue supper tasted so appetising: the ash-coated sausages were charred to a turn: there was a rich, earthy flavour about the cocoa warmed in the embers, fragments of which could be seen floating about on the surface of the lukewarm liquid. And everyone agreed that it was a treat to sink one's teeth into the brick-hard potatoes—and a problem to get them out again afterwards!

The guests wisely declined second helpings of the refreshments, but dug down deeply into pockets and purses at the rattling approach of the collecting tins . . . And when it was all over, the fire burnt out and the fireworks spent, the guests drove off in their cars and the boys trooped back indoors well satisfied with the evening's programme.

The members of the Form 3 Fireworks Fund had more reason than most for feeling pleased and proud with the results of the entertainment they had taken such trouble to devise. When the collectors had finished emptying their cocoa tins on the table in Classroom 3, the hon. treasurer was able to announce that, even allowing for the fact that his arithmetic wasn't very good, the sum of roughly five pounds had been raised for the cause of famine relief.

"Not bad, eh!" Jennings observed to his sub-committee as Martin-Jones gathered up the contributions to take to Mr. Carter's room for a more accurate reckoning. "I said we could have our fireworks and help the fund at the same time, didn't I!"

The self-appointed ginger-group grinned and nodded in agreement. "Trust Jennings!" the grins were meant to imply . . . Admittedly, the bonfire project had not gone exactly as planned but, all the same, November the fifth had certainly been a night to remember!

CHAPTER 11

Transport Problem

IN SPITE OF THE FACT that mathematics was not his best subject, Martin-Jones wasn't far out in his reckoning of the amount collected round the bonfire. When the total had been checked by Mr. Carter, it was found that the Form 3 Fireworks Fund had been able to contribute the sum of four pounds, ninety-two pence to the cause of famine relief.

"And that's not counting the twenty-three pence we collected in the village last Saturday," Atkinson remarked when the official figures reached Dormitory 4 just before lights out. "I reckon we've done our whack for Sir's fund for this term, at any rate."

Jennings didn't agree. "We ought to try and double it," he said.

"How?" asked Temple. "We can't have another Guy Fawkes collection till this time next year."

"No, but we could do something else. Like, say, for instance—" Jennings pulled a face and went on undressing. It was late in the evening and the atmosphere was still charged with the exciting memory of the bonfire. You couldn't expect a chap to produce brilliant brainwaves on the spur of the moment, he thought. Aloud, he said: "Leave it to me. I'll give my think-tank a stir and see what comes up to the top."

On Thursday, Miss Thorpe telephoned the headmaster to report that she had accidentally left her umbrella at the school after the fireworks celebrations.

"It's not a very valuable one, of course," she twittered into the telephone at full volume, while Mr. Pemberton-Oakes sat holding the receiver a foot away from his ear. "But if you should happen to come across it, I should be more than grateful if you would let me know. I'm almost sure I left it by the radiator in the drawing-room. Or, if not there, it could be on the table in the hall. Or it might even, perhaps, be worth looking under the—"

"That's all right, Miss Thorpe. We'll have a good look round for it," the headmaster promised, massaging his left ear which had taken the brunt of her full-throated bird-song. "I'll get one of the boys to bring it along to the cottage as soon as we find it."

The umbrella was nowhere to be found in the building despite a thorough search carried out by Robinson and other members of the domestic staff. But after football on Saturday, Binns and Blotwell discovered it by chance in the long grass near the pavilion where its owner had dropped it returning from the bonfire.

"Hey! Wow! Look what I've found!" cried Binns. He opened the umbrella and walked round with mincing steps holding an imaginary ankle-length skirt clear of the puddles.

Blotwell didn't think much of the female impersonation. "You look like a crab with chilblains," he said. "Bags we keep it, though. We could try out our famous wheeze now, couldn't we!"

The youngest boys hadn't heard about Miss Thorpe's loss and couldn't think why anyone should choose to abandon an umbrella in such an unlikely spot. All the same, they were delighted with their discovery, for it meant that they could now perform an experiment which they had often wanted to try, but had never before had the equipment to carry out.

"Gosh, yes, of course! Operation Airborne Earwigs!" Binns cried excitedly. "We'll have a bash with the umbrella first to see if it works, and then round up some recruits."

The two boys raced indoors and up the stairs towards Dormitory 2 on the top floor of the building; but as they were ascending the final fllight they met Mr. Pemberton-Oakes proceeding in the opposite direction.

"Ah! So the elusive umbrella has come to light," he said as he caught sight of the object which Binns was attempting to conceal behind his back. "I've no doubt that Miss Thorpe will be most relieved."

Binns didn't know what the headmaster was talking about, so he said: "It's just an old umbrella that we found by the pavilion, sir. We—er—we thought, perhaps, we ought to hand it in to lost property."

"Highly commendable!" the headmaster approved. "But the lost property cupboard happens to be on the ground floor, so may one inquire why you are taking the umbrella up to your dormitory?"

The two youngest boys looked sheepish and shuffled their feet. Blotwell said: "We were going to throw it out of the window, sir."

"You were going to do *what*?" Mr. Pemberton-Oakes raised a surprised eyebrow. He was aware that boys often did extraordinary things for reasons which seemed baffling to the average adult.

But this was carrying matters to extremes! He himself—even when young—had never been obsessed with the urge to throw umbrellas out of top-storey windows and he was curious to know what Binns and Blotwell were hoping to achieve by such a bizarre exploit. "May I ask why?" he inquired.

"Well, sir, we wanted to open it out and see whether

it dropped straight down like a pancake or glided down slowly like a parachute."

"Purely as a scientific experiment, I presume?"

"Well, yes, in a way, sir. You see, Binns and I thought that if we got something that didn't weigh very much like, say, some earwigs in a matchbox, and tied it on to the handle, we could let them do parachute descents."

"We shouldn't let them get hurt, sir," Binns hastened to assure him. "One of us was going to stand down below with a butterfly net to catch them if the umbrella came down too fast and—"

Mr. Pemberton-Oakes held up a restraining hand. Valuable though the experiment might be for the advancement of aeronautical research, he had other things to do besides listening to an account of the safety precautions to be adopted on behalf of the parachuting earwigs.

"Take the umbrella to Mr. Carter and ask him to see that it's returned to Miss Thorpe," the headmaster commanded.

"Yes, sir!"

As they went down the stairs, he found himself mentally toying with the problem they had been hoping to solve. Would the umbrella descend like a parachute or like a pancake? . . . H'm! Assuming the weight of the object was approximately half a kilogram, and the diameter when extended was roughly a metre; then, with a light south-westerly breeze blowing at a speed of— Mr. Pemberton-Oakes pulled himself together with a blink of reproach. "This is ridiculous!" he thought. "I'm getting as bad as the boys!"

Binns and Blotwell found Mr. Carter on the front steps surrounded by a group of boys applying for village leave. This privilege did not extend to Form 1, and the two youngest boys had difficulty in pushing their way through the crowd to reach the master on duty.

"It's the Head's special orders," Binns insisted at the top of his voice when curtly rebuked by his elders for intruding. "Blotters and I have been specially picked to take an urgent and confidential message to Sir."

Mr. Carter rescued the special messengers and listened to their urgent tidings. Then he said to the rest of the group: "Do any of you boys know where Oaktree Cottage is?"

Jennings and Darbishire raised their hands. "We do, sir. We've been there before."

"Right!" Mr. Carter handed the umbrella to Jennings. "Take this to Miss Thorpe with the headmaster's compliments."

"Yes, sir."

"And come straight back," the master continued, remembering Mr. Wilkins' complaints of the previous week. "I don't want a repetition of the sort of thing that happened the last time you had village leave."

Jennings and Darbishire set off across the field-path to Linbury, Jennings twirling the umbrella and tossing it high into the air like a drum-major leading a band.

"Hey, you're supposed to be delivering this gadget in one piece," Darbishire said when the drum-major dropped his catch for the fourth time.

Jennings retrieved the umbrella from a wheel-rut and wiped the mud off with a dockleaf.

"She won't mind. She's quite a decent old stick really," he said. "We'd have been in dead trouble with Old Wilkie last week if she hadn't taken our side."

Oaktree Cottage stood in a tidy garden near the centre of the village. The house was very old and very small, with an expanse of tiled roof sloping almost to the ground on one side. There were frail-looking bow windows to catch the sun, and a solid oak front door studded with huge nails which looked secure enough to serve as the portal of a prison.

Miss Thorpe saw her visitors at the gate and came out to meet them as they were coming up the path.

"So you've found my umbrella! How perfectly splendid! And how kind of you to bring it all the way down to the cottage," she chirruped.

Jennings presented it to her with the headmaster's compliments. "We raised just on five pounds at the bonfire," he added proudly. "I was hoping we might be able to double it, but I haven't had the right sort of brainwave yet."

They declined her offer of a cup of tea, but readily accepted her invitation to take a bag of apples back to school to share with their friends.

"Come along to the barn and we'll pick some out," she said, leading the way down the garden path. "I've grown some beauties this year, and the barn's so cool and dry they're as perfect as when they came off the tree."

Miss Thorpe's barn at the end of her garden was a small, thatched out-building about half the size of her cottage.

Inside, it looked like a junk shop for, in addition to the garden produce stored on the shelves, there was a quantity of old-fashioned furniture for which she could find no room elsewhere. Amongst the *bric-à-brac* were an ancient mangle with huge wooden rollers, a knife-grinding machine, an old gramophone, an oil-cooker and a small cottage piano.

The boys looked about them with mild curiosity

while Miss Thorpe was picking out the choicest apples from her store.

"Funny place to keep a piano," Jennings remarked. He opened the lid of the instrument, pressed one of the keys and saw a small black beetle emerge from the woodwork and set off on a walk along the keyboard.

"I've no room for it indoors, so it just has to stay out here gathering cobwebs," Miss Thorpe replied. "I'd willingly give it away if I knew of someone who really needed it."

Darbishire wasn't used to generosity on this scale. "*Give* it away!" he echoed in surprise. "Free of charge, do you mean?"

"Well, it's no use to me, eating its head off in the barn. Unfortunately, I don't play the piano myself, and I'm sure nobody would want to buy it." She finished sorting out the apples and handed the bag to Darbishire. "I've asked one or two people in the village if they'd like it, but they're all so busy watching television every evening that nobody seems to need a piano any more."

Jennings was unusually silent as the boys followed their hostess back along the garden path. But when they reached the gate he turned to her and said: "Excuse me, Miss Thorpe, but if you *really* don't want that old piano of yours, I know somebody who would be jolly pleased to have it."

She looked at him inquiringly. "And who is that?"

"Me!"

Darbishire was so flabbergasted that he nearly dropped the bag of apples. "You! You must be off your runners, Jen!" he protested. "What do *you* want a piano for? We've got about six up at school already. And anyway, where would you keep it?

In your boot-locker? In your sponge-bag? Where?"

Jennings silenced the facetious criticism with a withering look. "I don't want it for *myself*," he said with dignity. "I want it for famine relief. I've been trying to think all the week how we could double that five pounds we collected, and I reckon I've found the answer."

They looked at him without understanding.

"You'll never sell it, if that's what you mean," Miss Thorpe insisted. "I'm sure no dealer would give so much as a 'thank you' for an out-of-date cottage piano like mine."

The boy's tone was earnest, but his eyes sparkled with excitement as he said: "Ah, yes, Miss Thorpe, but I know something that you don't know! There's a music shop in Dunhambury which positively guarantees to give you at least five pounds—five pounds and upwards, it says—for old, second-hand pianos."

Darbishire laughed. "Perhaps they're joking!"

"*Joking!*" Jennings was incensed at his friend's disbelief. "I've seen it with my own eyes, I tell you! *In writing!* I saw it from the bus when we went to Bracebridge and I saw it again when I went to have my hair cut that time." He paused, and prodded Darbishire in the chest to underline the gravity of his statement. "They wouldn't *dare* to put a notice like that in the window if they didn't mean what they said. You could have them up for fraud!"

Miss Thorpe was impressed with the sincerity of the boy's manner. "It's quite possible, of course," she conceded. "There may be a rising demand for second-hand pianos—especially antique models like mine: but it's been in the barn so long that it's not in very good order, I'm afraid."

"That doesn't matter," Jennings assured her. "The notice definitely said *in any condition*. That means we could get five pounds for it even if—if—" He searched his mind for a telling example. "—even if black beetles come belting out of the cracks and run up and down the keyboard every time you play *God Save the Queen*."

"Well, there's no harm in trying. I'm all in favour if the money can be used to benefit a good cause," Miss Thorpe agreed. "I think you'd better come indoors and have a cup of tea after all, so we can discuss the best way of going about it."

Over a cup of tea, they hammered out *The Plan of the Antique Piano* © *Copyright by J. C. T. Jennings, with acknowledgments to F. Thorpe and C. Darbishire.*

They would take the instrument to the Dunhambury music shop the following Saturday afternoon, they decided, provided that they could solve the problem of how to get it there. Miss Thorpe had a car which she was willing to use, but it wasn't the sort of vehicle which could be employed to transport a piano.

"Not even a *small* piano," she insisted as they knitted their brows over the first snag on their list. "Mind you, I *have* got a towing-bar on the back—on the back of the car, I mean, not on the back of the piano: it was already fitted when I bought the car second-hand last year. So what we really need is a trailer."

Jennings and Darbishire exchanged hopeful glances. Mr. Pemberton-Oakes had a trailer and was the obvious person to approach. But would he agree to lend it? The chances were that he would put his foot down firmly at the very idea of his junior boys hawking beetle-ridden pianos up and down Dunhambury High Street on a busy Saturday afternoon.

"I think it would be better if *you* asked him rather

than us," Darbishire said with a persuasive smile when the headmaster's name was mentioned. "He might not take any notice of Jen and me, but he couldn't very well say no to a grown-up person like you."

"Not if you wrap it up in a lot of old flannel about wanting to borrow it for famine relief," Jennings put in. His mind leaped ahead, considering possible complications. "But when you ask him, it would be better not to say too much about Darbishire and me, because we're not supposed to go farther than Linbury on village leave. Just tell him that you want us to bring the trailer along to your cottage. That'll explain things nicely as far as the Head needs to know."

Miss Thorpe was by no means willing to enter into a conspiracy—whether it was wrapped up in old flannel or not. All the same, she agreed to telephone Mr. Pemberton-Oakes and ask his permission for the boys to help in the venture. She would explain the whole situation, and leave it to him to make the decision. There was really no reason why he should refuse, she told them. She was merely seeking his co-operation in what was, after all, a truly worthwhile cause.

The boys were late in arriving back at school and Mr. Carter demanded explanations.

"Miss Thorpe kept us, sir," Jennings informed him. "She insisted on taking us indoors and giving us cups of tea and apples and things, and we couldn't very well get away until she'd finished talking. It wouldn't have been polite, would it, sir?"

Mr. Carter accepted the excuse with a wan smile and the traditional pinch of salt. It was his own fault for choosing those particular boys for an errand of that nature, he thought . . . . Trust Jennings to make the most of it!

CHAPTER 12

Double Yellow Line

MR. PEMBERTON-OAKES was out when Miss Thorpe telephoned the school on Monday and the call was taken by Mrs. Hackett, one of the cleaners who happened to be dusting his study at the time. Upon his return he found a note on his message pad which read: *Miss Thorpe phoned to say she has good cause and wants Jennings, Darbishire and Taylor for Saturday afternoon.*

The headmaster was puzzled. There was no boy in the school named Taylor. He was about to ring Oaktree Cottage and ask for more precise information when Jennings arrived at the study with Form 3's Latin books which he had been detailed to collect for marking.

"Your name is mentioned in a somewhat cryptic message I have received from Miss Thorpe," the headmaster said, as the boy put the pile of books down on the leather-topped desk. "Perhaps you can shed some light on the mystery."

"Cryptic message, sir?" the boy queried. "I haven't done anything cryptic—honestly, sir. I don't even know what it means."

"You misunderstand me. I meant merely that some form of secret code seems to have been employed," Mr. Pemberton-Oakes explained. "Otherwise, I am rather at a loss to understand why she should have good cause for wanting you and Darbishire—not to mention the non-existent Taylor—on Saturday afternoon."

He passed the message pad across the desk. Jennings studied it, frowning, for some seconds. Then his eyes lit up with inspiration.

"I've got it, sir! I've solved it! It's meant to be *trailer*, not Taylor. She wants to borrow your trailer in a good cause."

The headmaster nodded. It wasn't the first time that Miss Thorpe had approached him with a similar sort of request.

"It's all to do with raising money for charity," the boy went on. "You see, when we took her umbrella back, she gave us some apples and told us all about it. And we offered to help and push the trailer for her, if you'd very kindly give us permission, sir."

"I see!" The request seemed reasonable, now that the contents of the message had been made clear. Miss Thorpe was well known for her fund-raising activities and was obviously proposing to sell garden produce, or something of the sort, for charitable purposes. The trailer would be most useful for transporting her wares around the village.

"Very well, then, Jennings. I see no reason why you shouldn't lend a hand in pushing the trailer."

"Thank you, sir. Thank you very much. And Darbishire, too, sir?"

"By all means, Darbishire too! In fact, I think it may well need three or four boys to control the trailer when it's loaded with—ah—boxes of apples or whatever it is that Miss Thorpe wants it for." The headmaster beamed a look of approval across the leather-topped desk. "You'd better get hold of a couple more boys to go with you. You can tell the master on duty that you have my permission."

Jennings left the study well satisfied with the way in which the plan was taking shape. Darbishire must be kept informed of the latest developments, he thought, so he hurried off to the common-room where he found his friend arranging his stamp album during the after-lunch rest period.

"It's all right, Darbi! The Head's given us per for next Saturday," Jennings announced as he came into the room. "And we can rope in a couple of chaps to help us too."

Darbishire was amazed. "You mean he said 'yes', without even batting an eyelid? He doesn't mind us trundling a moth-eaten, beetle-ridden old piano round Dunhambury?"

"He doesn't actually *know* about the piano—or about Dunhambury either," Jennings admitted, lowering his voice for security reasons. "You see, he wasn't in when Miss Thorpe rang up, and for some reason he seems to think she needs the trailer to carry apples round the village on."

"Apples? Where did he get that idea from?"

Jennings shrugged. "Well, I did try to explain after a fashion, but he didn't ask for details, so I didn't give him any."

"Much safer," his friend agreed. "You can't go *on* explaining things to grown-ups if they can't be bothered to listen. It isn't your fault if he's jumped to the wrong conclusion."

The next item on the agenda was to enlist a couple of boys to help with the trailer, so Jennings made his way over to Temple and Venables who were playing chess in a far corner of the room. They were only too willing to help when they heard what the project involved, but—like Darbishire—they were anxious to know whether the headmaster's permission had been obtained.

"Well, it has—*sort of*," Jennings told them. "He knows we're going off to do good works with Miss Thorpe, but after that it's a bit dodgy. He mustn't know the details or he might stop it, so we'll have to make it a top-security hush-hush mission."

Venables said: "How are you going to get the piano on to the trailer?"

Jennings hadn't thought of that. It was only a small piano, admittedly, but even so, it would be far beyond the strength of the four boys to lift it unaided.

"Pity we can't get hold of a fork-lift truck," said Temple.

"*Fork* lift!" Venables echoed. "What we need is a *piano* lift. We'd hardly need a truck to lift forks."

"Very funny! Hilarious joke!" Temple said shortly. "All the same, Jen, it's a problem. You'd better start feeding the data into your old think-tank and see if it comes up with an answer."

So that evening Jennings posted a letter to Oaktree Cottage. It said:

Dear Miss Thorpe,

We have got per to come plus the trailer plus two more to help push. But we think it will be too heavy to get up, so have you got any men we could have to help get it up, or we shall have trouble getting it up as it is so heavy. If you can think of something do not telephone your answer as it may fall into the wrong hands!

I hope you are having good weather,

Yours truly,

J. C. T. Jennings.

"It doesn't seem all that clear to me," Darbishire said as he read the letter over his friend's shoulder. "The way you put it she may think the school telephone has been bugged."

"We'll have to risk that. I daren't put any more in a letter in case *that* falls into the wrong hands too!"

Whether or not Miss Thorpe was impressed by the need for secrecy, she at least heeded the warning about maintaining telephonic silence. She, too, had been worried about the problem of lifting the piano, so the following day she went to Arrowsmith's farm and had a word with the farmer whom she knew well.

The result was that when Jennings and his trailer-crew arrived at Oaktree Cottage shortly after two o'clock on Saturday, they found three burly farm-workers chatting to their hostess outside the gate.

"Ah! Here comes the trailer! Splendid!" she chirped like a lark greeting a spring morning. "Wheel it along to the barn, boys!" She waved a hand towards the farmworkers by way of introduction. "Barney, Rocker and Mr. Fouracres have kindly come along to lend a hand with the loading."

Rocker, a sturdy, bare-headed youth in jeans and gumboots, said: "How do!" The other two nodded and stamped out the stubs of their home-rolled cigarettes.

"*So* good of Mr. Oakes to let you come," Miss Thorpe went on as she followed the trailer down the garden path. "I wasn't able to speak to him myself on the telephone, but I left a very clear message so that he would know exactly what we were planning to do."

Jennings suppressed a smile. Now that they were safely away from the school premises there was nothing to worry about, he thought. . . . It was as well for his peace of mind that he was unaware of the headmaster's engagements for the later part of the afternoon.

The farmworkers had no difficulty in lifting the piano on to the trailer. Mr. Fouracres, a large man in a donkey jacket and a woollen cap, took hold of one end of the instrument, while Rocker helped Barney, the eldest and gloomiest of the trio, to lift the other. The boys were not needed for the loading and had little to do besides holding the trailer steady.

Then, with the piano lying on its back, the farmworkers wheeled the trailer out to the road and attached it to the towing-bar of Miss Thorpe's car.

"Thank you, thank you, that's splendid," Miss Thorpe twittered when the job was done. She opened the car door and called to the boys: "Jump in! All aboard and away we go!"

The car drove off in the direction of Dunhambury, while the farmworkers stood watching by the gate. Mr. Fouracres looked at Barney and said: "All very well getting us to lift it on for them. How d'you reckon they're going to get it off again at the other end?"

Barney scratched his ear thoughtfully. "Ah! That's a real old puzzler, that is!" He shrugged. "None of our business, though!"

Miss Thorpe drove slowly and with extreme care. She was not used to towing a trailer, she told the boys, and felt sure they would understand her anxiety for the safety of her passengers and the survival of her load.

It took twenty-five minutes to cover the five miles to Dunhambury, but at last they reached the town and joined the steady stream of vehicles crawling up the busy High Street.

Jennings, seated next to the driver, was on the lookout for the music shop.

"There it is! Just across the road, look!" he cried suddenly, pointing through the windscreen. "And it's still got the notice in the window. Goodo!" He turned to the driver. "Will you stop over there, please, Miss Thorpe. Just past that lamp-post on the other side of the road."

The car was moving forward in an unbroken line of vehicles, with a post office van just in front and a milk lorry close behind.

"I can't stop now! And I certainly can't get across the road—it's out of the question!" Miss Thorpe protested. It was typical of a non-driver to make such an impossible demand without warning, she thought. "There's a lorry on my tail and all sorts of things coming towards me."

"But we've *got* to stop! If we go past the shop we'll have to lug the piano all the way back, and we'll never manage it by ourselves."

"Tut! This is most awkward! Still, I'll do my best," the driver agreed, edging the car towards the middle of the road. "But really, this is a hopeless place to try to stop."

"It's double yellow line all the way up the street," Darbishire pointed out from the rear seat.

"And there's a traffic warden on the corner, too," said Venables.

"We shan't stop for long. I'll rush into the shop and get the piano men to come out and lift it off for us," Jennings told them. "As soon as they've got it off the trailer, Miss Thorpe can drive off and find somewhere to park and then walk back and join us."

It sounded a feasible suggestion, but unfortunately it made no allowance for the heavy volume of traffic passing up and down Dunhambury High Street on a busy Saturday afternoon.

Miss Thorpe flicked her off-side indicator and pulled up in the middle of the road, to the annoyance of the driver of the milk lorry who was unable to get past.

By the time there was a gap in the approaching traffic, the queue behind the milk lorry stretched all the way down to the traffic lights at the bottom of the hill. Pink to the ears with embarrassment, Miss Thorpe drove across to the off-side pavement and, ignoring the double yellow lines, stopped the car alongside the kerb.

Jennings jumped out and raced into the music shop, while the other boys climbed out of the back and gathered on the pavement beside the trailer.

The traffic warden arrived as Miss Thorpe was getting out of the driving-seat. He was a thin, rather unhappy-looking man with a tired voice.

"You can't stop here," he announced. "Double yellow line."

"Yes, yes, I know. But I've no intention of parking, I assure you," Miss Thorpe answered. "Just getting something off the trailer, that's all."

The warden shook his head. "Not here, you're not! Double yellow line."

"But surely I can stop long enough to unload my trailer. I'm delivering a piano to the music shop."

"Double yellow line," he repeated.

"I know that. But I've often seen lorries delivering goods to the shops along here."

The warden shook his head. "Not on Saturday afternoons, you haven't. Not along the double yellow."

Miss Thorpe was in a quandary. Legally, she hadn't a leg to stand on. But surely, she reasoned, this was a situation in which common sense should prevail. Double yellow lines or not, she really ought to be allowed to get the piano off the trailer.

She turned to the warden to plead her cause, and at that moment Jennings emerged, alone, from the music shop and joined his companions on the pavement.

"It's hopeless!" he told them. "There's only one assistant in there and he's serving a customer. He wouldn't take any notice when I said it was urgent."

"What are we going to do, then?" asked Temple.

"We'll have to try and get it off by ourselves. Perhaps we could slide it. I'll undo the trailer, while you chaps let down the tail-board and try and get the piano upright as it comes off. If we can once get it on its casters we'll be able to push it about quite easily."

"Yes, but what if—" Darbishire began.

"No time to argue. The warden's getting impatient." Jennings went to the rear of the car and called out: "Ready! Stand by for action!"

So saying, he jerked the split-pin out of its spindle and heaved with all his strength, while Darbishire let down the tail-board. Released from the towing-bar, the shaft of the trailer shot upwards while the other end, weighed down by its load, descended with a loud thump. . . . The piano slid down off the trailer, out of control, and lay on its back in the roadway. Small black beetles ran out of the woodwork and scurried about in all directions.

Jennings was furious. "What did you want to let it go so fast for! You were supposed to be holding it upright."

"I'd like to see you do better!" Temple grumbled. "We hadn't got a chance to steady it. It came down with a swoosh."

Darbishire said: "Let's not argue. We're in real trouble now!"

They certainly were!

Alarmed by the thump, the traffic warden broke off his argument with Miss Thorpe and swung round to see what was amiss.

"Cor! Stone the crows!" he cried in exasperation. "Perishing pianos all over the road! Cars and trailers all along the double yellow! Get this vehicle out of this street, quick, or we'll be blocked solid from here to Brighton!"

It was obvious that frail little Miss Thorpe was quite incapable of hitching up the trailer unaided, so the warden grabbed hold of the shaft and did it for her. Then he opened up a gap in the traffic through which she managed to squeeze both car and trailer back on to the proper side of the road.

She gave the boys an encouraging wave as she drove off to find a car park.

"Do not despair!" the wave was meant to imply. "I'll be back when I've found somewhere to park!"

CHAPTER 13

Honky-tonk

As soon as Miss Thorpe had driven away, the traffic warden turned his attention to the piano lying in the roadway and blocking the flow of traffic down the hill.

"Cor! This is a right creamer! Somebody's going to pay for this," he threatened. His voice was no longer tired and his unhappy look had been replaced by an expression of baffled fury. "That woman's asking for a summons, the trouble she's caused, and you boys are an absolute menace. Look at the traffic! Building up five miles each way, I shouldn't wonder."

"We're terribly sorry," Jennings apologised. "It was that stupid man in the music shop. He wouldn't come out and help!"

A crowd had collected on the pavement and the warden beckoned to a few of the spectators to come to his assistance.

"Give us a hand getting this thing up," he requested. "Can't leave it here, blocking the road."

With the help of the bystanders, the little piano was raised upright and set down on the pavement clear of the traffic.

"Thanks ever so much, everybody," Jennings said with a nervous smile. "We can manage on our own now we've got it on its casters. Nothing more to worry about."

The traffic warden snorted. "I'm glad *somebody's* got nothing to worry about," he muttered as he hurried off to sort out the tangle of traffic farther up the hill.

The spectators dispersed and the four boys wheeled their cargo across the pavement to the door of the shop. Whatever musical qualities the piano may have lacked, the casters at the base of the instrument were in perfect condition.

"Are you sure they'll be interested?" Temple asked Jennings when they reached the doorway. "You said the chap wouldn't listen when you went in just now."

"Ah, that was because he was busy with a customer and didn't want to be interrupted. It'll be all right now, though. After all—" Jennings pointed to the notice in the window. "Five pounds and upwards, it says. They can't very well get round that, can they!"

In order to get the instrument through the shop door, Jennings and Darbishire pulled at one end while Venables and Temple pushed at the other. When half the piano was over the threshold and the other half outside on the pavement, progress was arrested by the arrival of the shop assistant, who came hurrying out of a back room to find out what was happening.

He was a small, rather aggressive man, wearing thick horn-rimmed glasses and a shabby blue suit. "What's this, then! What's going on!" he demanded.

Jennings greeted him with a disarming smile. "Good afternoon," he said politely. "We saw your notice in the window about buying pianos, so we've brought one to sell you." He indicated the instrument in the doorway. "It isn't a terribly good one, I'm afraid, but your notice does say 'in any condition'."

The salesman looked at him sharply. "Are you lads on your own, or is there a grown-up with you?"

"Oh, we've got a grown-up—Miss Thorpe," Jennings explained. "She's gone off to park the car, but she'll be back soon. You see, the warden wouldn't let her stop and you didn't come and help, so we've had to bring it in by ourselves."

The little man nodded. "And this lady wants to buy a new one, does she?"

"Oh, no, she doesn't want to *buy* a piano—she can't even play. She wants to sell one for famine relief."

With a slight shrug, the salesman turned away. "No good coming here, then. We only take old pianos in part-exchange for new ones."

Jennings' jaw dropped and he stared at the man in dismay. "Part-exchange!" he echoed. "But what about that notice in your window?"

"Yes, *what* about it?" Darbishire cried, horrified at this setback to their plans. "It says it in black and white—in writing. You can't get away from that!"

The little man's aggressive manner softened and he heaved a long and patient sigh. He had met optimists like these boys before.

"Listen, son," he said, pointing a bony forefinger at Darbishire. "We get snowed under with people like you wanting to make a bit of money out of worm-ridden old pianos that are only fit for the scrap-heap. It's no good bringing that sort of garbage to us."

"But it says *in any condition*," Jennings reminded him.

"Oh, we'd *take* it all right—in part-exchange," the assistant agreed. "When a genuine customer comes in with a barrow-load of rubbish like that,"—he switched his pointing forefinger to the instrument stuck in the doorway—"we sell him a new one and send the old crock to the corporation refuse dump."

Jennings felt cheated. "You should say what you

mean. Your notice is a fraud," he said accusingly.

"Of course it isn't. If somebody wants to do a deal, it's worth our while to take his junk and knock five pounds off the price of a new model for a quick sale. That's why it has to be part-exchange, see. These old things are no use to us. We can't even give them away— let alone sell them!"

Suddenly the bottom had fallen out of *The Plan of the Antique Piano*. Jennings could have wept with frustration: the brilliant brainwave, the careful planning, the hazards faced and overcome—all these counted for nothing. The project was an utter failure.

He turned to his companion and said: "Come on, Darbi. We'd better go and tell the others. They'll be wondering what's happening."

Venables and Temple, hopping about impatiently outside the shop, were certainly wondering what had been happening. They could see their spokesman talking to the shop assistant, but the rumble of passing traffic prevented them from hearing what was being said.

They had made an attempt to follow their companions into the shop, but the piano had been taking up so much space that they hadn't been able to squeeze past. But now, hopeful that the deal was all but completed, they craned their necks round the obstruction in the doorway, demanding information.

"Got the money, Jen?" Temple sang out.

"How much did he give you?" demanded Venables.

Jennings spread out his hands in a gesture of despair. "Nothing! It's all a wash-out. He won't buy it."

"Won't buy it!" Venables echoed in shocked surprise. "But he *must* buy it. We can't take it all the way back again! It's not possible."

There was some truth in Venables' remark. Without the three farmworkers to do the lifting, the prospect of reloading the piano on to the trailer was enough to make the mind boggle with apprehension.

There would be chaos in the High Street. In his mind's eye, Jennings could picture the traffic jammed solid in all directions: the futile efforts of Miss Thorpe to park the trailer outside the shop: the fury of the traffic warden at yet another breach of the regulations about double yellow lines!

He turned back to the salesman and said: "I'm awfully sorry, but I'm afraid we shall have to leave it here. There's nothing else we can do with it."

The salesman bridled indignantly and his aggressive manner reasserted itself. "I'll tell you what you can do with it," he said angrily. "You can take it out of this shop. I'm not having that heap of old firewood cluttering the place up, spreading woodworm, and all. Get it out of here at once!"

"But where can we put it? We can't just dump it in the street."

"Oh, yes, we *can* dump it in the street, and I'll show you how we're going to do it." The salesman swept past the boys, put his shoulder to the protruding end of the piano and pushed with all his strength.

Venables and Temple leaped for safety as the instrument came bumping over the doormat towards them and slid to rest on the pavement outside.

"There you are! It's all yours now, mate. I've finished with it—and with you, too!" the assistant panted, as Jennings and Darbishire followed their unwanted property through the door. "And if it's still there in ten minutes' time I shall phone the police and get you run in for obstructing my windows." He strode back into the shop and slammed the door behind him.

The boys stood on the pavement in utter dejection.

"What on earth are we going to do!" bemoaned Temple.

"If only Miss Thorpe would come back," sighed Darbishire, looking up and down the street. "How much longer is she going to be, parking that car?"

Jennings shook his head and pulled a long face. There wasn't much Miss Thorpe would be able to do about it, he reflected bitterly, as the shopping crowds swirled past or stopped to gape at the unhappy quartet and their pathetic piano .... This, he felt, was one of those hopeless situations from which there was no escape!

It was the custom of Ronald Alfred Hales, senior assistant at Walton's Men's Hairdressing Saloon (Established 1929), to stroll along the High Street during his afternoon tea-break to enjoy a much-needed pot of tea and two slices of toast at Ye Olde Tudor Bunne Shoppe (Established 1969), halfway down the hill.

It would have to be a quick "cuppa" today, he reminded himself as he crossed at the traffic lights: the saloon had been busy since dinner-time, and what with customers coming in and demanding— His train of thought stopped with a jolt as he drew level with the music shop and found his progress impeded by a small cottage piano taking up half the width of the pavement.

Mr. Hales glanced up and saw four Linbury Court boys standing round it, submerged in gloom. One of them he recognised as the boy who had come into the saloon more than a fortnight earlier, seeking treatment after his accident with the paint spray.

"Hallo, hallo! Doing your music practice out in the street!" Mr. Hales said in flippant greeting. "Not thinking of giving the old ivories a coat of aluminium paint, are you!"

His jocular tone found no answering echo in the worried voice of the leader of the group who looked up and said: "It's no laughing matter, Mr. Hales. We've got to get rid of this piano somehow, or we may be arrested for obstruction."

"Goodness me! What's been going on, then?"

Mr. Hales listened to their story with a suitably grave expression. When it was over he said: "Tut! You don't half go around asking for trouble. I've never met such a lad for sticking his neck out." He frowned in thought and tapped the piano with his finger. "If you want to get rid of it, it's just possible that young Andy Chester is still on the look-out for an old box of tricks like this."

"Andy Chester?" The name meant nothing to Jennings.

"He runs the Youth Club in Denton Street. They were after an old piano for a revue they're putting on, but it may be too late by now."

The boys clutched at this straw of hope. "Let's go and ask him," Venables cried eagerly. "Where did you say he lived?"

Mr. Hales considered for a moment and decided to forgo his tea-break in a good cause. "I'll take you round," he offered.

"But what about the piano? How are we going to get it there?" Darbishire asked.

"On its casters, of course," the hairdresser replied. "It's only just round the first corner and it's downhill most of the way."

The sight of four boys and one elderly man pushing

a piano along the pavement caused several of the Saturday afternoon shoppers to turn and stare. Politely, they stepped aside to allow the removal crew room to manœuvre, and then lost interest as the instrument was wheeled round the corner and disappeared from view.

Although situated close to the main thoroughfare, Denton Street was a quiet road, reasonably free from traffic. This was because it led nowhere in particular, and the knowing motorist could often find space to park his car in front of the dreary, terraced houses which ran along the street for most of its length.

At the far end of the street, where the houses stopped, was a corrugated-iron building, formerly a non-conformist chapel and now the headquarters of the Dunhambury Youth Club.

Here the removal crew stopped, and Mr. Hales, panting audibly, went into the building in search of the Youth Club leader.

"I hope he hasn't had a heart-attack," Temple said when five minutes had ticked away. "He was shoving like the back row of a rugger scrum getting it up the kerb just now; and you can tell he isn't used to it."

But a moment later Mr. Hales reappeared, accompanied by a genial, bearded young man in a vast sweater and faded fawn trousers.

"Sorry I was so long, lads. I had to phone the shop to say I'd be late back," the hairdresser explained. He indicated the young man by his side. "This is Andy Chester. I've told him all about it."

The Youth Club leader greeted the boys with a grin and cast an eye over the piano parked on the pavement.

"We'll see how it sounds first, shall we!" He threw

back the lid and, standing at the keyboard, struck a few
tentative chords at full volume.

Darbishire winced at the sound. It didn't need a keen
musical ear to detect that the moth-eaten felts had
worn away and that the wooden hammers were pounding unprotected strings. Surely Mr. Chester wouldn't
take a tinny old piano like this, even as a gift!

But the pianist had swung into a rousing melody
and was vamping out the tune with a look of ecstasy
on his face. When he got to the end he turned to the
boys, beaming with delight.

"Gorgeous! Absolutely gorgeous! A real, genuine,
vintage, died-in-the-wool honky-tonk," he exclaimed.
"You can never really get this fruity, metallic sound
by tinkering with an *ordinary* piano. It's like wine—the
tone needs time to mature."

The boys looked at him in some surprise. "You mean
you'll take it?" Jennings asked.

"You bet I'll take it! I've been searching for weeks
for a piano that sounds as though it's mixing cement
while you're playing it. It's just what we need for our
revue." Mr. Chester's smile grew wider: his voice was
vibrant with enthusiasm. "We've written it ourselves,
you know. It's called *Through Darkest Dunhambury*, and
we don't half take the mickey at some of the local
bigwigs. For instance, there's one scene—"

He broke off as a group of teenage boys and girls
came swinging along the street, talking amongst themselves in loud and lively voices. One of the older boys
was carrying a trumpet, and a girl had a guitar slung
over her shoulder.

"Some of the cast. We've got a rehearsal this afternoon," Andy Chester explained, and then shouted
down the street: "Hey, listen, you cloth-eared lot!

How about this for a rattling tin-can piano backing!"

Again he started to pound out the lively melody, and the teenage group swarmed round the piano, tapping their feet to the rhythm and listening with every sign of approval. The girl with the guitar took up the accompaniment and the youth with the trumpet joined in. Somebody fetched a chair for the pianist from the club premises. The music grew louder, the rest of the group took up their cue and started dancing and, with startling suddenness, a spontaneous rehearsal was taking place up and down the pavement and over-flowing on to the road.

Jennings and his companions watched in spellbound wonder. This was something new and exciting—something outside the normal experience of those who spent their lives complying with the demands of boarding-school routine. Already they had forgotten their frus-trating encounter with the man in the music shop: they had forgotten Miss Thorpe as well, and were too enthralled with the entertainment to spare a thought for the fact that she might be looking for them.

A small crowd gathered, attracted by the sound of the music, and people were peeping out through the lace-curtained windows of the terraced houses. Such goings-on were unheard of in Denton Street!

Mr. Hales, revelling in his unauthorised tea-break, touched Jennings on the arm and said: "Didn't you say you were doing this piano-selling lark for charity?"

The boy nodded. "That's right. Famine relief."

The hairdresser indicated the growing crowd with a sweep of his arm. "Here's your chance to make a bit, then! Pass the hat round while they're watching the dancing, and you'll be laughing all the way to the bank!"

It was a brilliant suggestion, but at first Jennings felt diffident about trespassing on the goodwill of the entertainers. "Do you think Mr. Chester would mind?" he asked uneasily.

"Good heavens, no! I know Andy. He'll be only too pleased to help."

Still Jennings hesitated. "But I haven't got my collecting-box any more."

"That's no excuse!" Mr. Hales jerked his thumb towards the premises behind them. "You'll find something in there you can use."

Darbishire had been following the conversation with interest. "It's a good idea, Jen. I'll come and help you," he offered.

Together the two boys went in through the open front door and found themselves in a large hall with a stage at one end. Nobody was about, but properties and scenery for the forthcoming production were scattered around the floor.

"How about this for raking in the money!" Darbishire suggested, picking up a battered bowler hat from a pile of theatrical costumes.

Jennings shook his head. It was too ludicrous for a serious project, he thought. He looked round and found an empty coffee tin on a window-ledge. "This'll be better," he decided. "And we ought to have a notice saying what we're collecting for."

Darbishire rose to the occasion. On the back of a cardboard poster advertising soft drinks he wrote the words *Support Famine Relief* with a scrap of chalk he found on the floor below the dartboard.

"It's a bit rough," Jennings admitted as they hurried out of the building with their equipment. "But I reckon they'll get the message all right."

The music had come to a stop by this time and the crowd were beginning to drift away. But as Jennings and Darbishire appeared, Mr. Hales signalled to them and went over to the Youth Club leader for a quick consultation.

Andy Chester nodded, rose to his feet and addressed the crowd. "Please don't go away, ladies and gentlemen," he called loudly. "By special request we are now going to present our spectacular finale. During this item a collection will be taken for the worthwhile cause of international famine relief."

The tinny piano twanged out its metallic notes, guitar and trumpet joined in, and the rest of the cast writhed to the rhythm and sang at the tops of their voices.

Mr. Hales was the first to drop a coin into the coffee tin. "I'm off now," he said. "You lads will get me shot, keeping me out of the shop for forty minutes on a Saturday afternoon."

They tried to thank him for what he had done but he wouldn't stop to listen. "That's all right," he called over his shoulder as he turned to go. "It's been a real tonic. I haven't enjoyed a tea-break like this for years."

The collectors picked their way slowly through the crowd, Jennings jingling his tin and Darbishire following with the written evidence to prove that the proceeds would be used to good purpose.

Most of the audience made some contribution and Jennings was overjoyed at the speed with which the coins came raining into the tin.

"Thank you . . . . Thank you!" he kept repeating as they worked their way through to the back of the crowd.

And then it happened!

He had turned to say something to Darbishire just behind him, and wasn't even looking at the prospective donor at whom he was automatically shaking his tin.

"Thank you . . . . Thank you!" But this time there was no response to his invitation, and Jennings glanced up at the tall figure in the grey overcoat standing before him.

His glance was returned by the cold, unwavering stare of M. W. B. Pemberton-Oakes, M.A., headmaster of Linbury Court School.

CHAPTER 14

Copyright Reserved

THE ENCOUNTER was so unexpected that for some moments Jennings and the headmaster stood staring at each other in surprise. As for Darbishire, he was so overcome with shock that the poster fell from his nerveless fingers and lay upside-down in the gutter at his feet.

Mr. Pemberton-Oakes was the first to recover the power of speech.

"Correct me if I'm wrong, Jennings," he said gently, "but I was under the impression that I gave you boys permission to help Miss Thorpe distribute garden produce in the village."

Jennings said nothing. The words wouldn't come.

"I am therefore at a loss to understand why I should find you holding a street collection in—ah—dubious circumstances in the middle of Dunhambury." The headmaster paused. "I await your reply with interest."

"Well, sir, perhaps we didn't make it quite clear," Jennings faltered. "You see, Miss Thorpe had got this piano that she didn't want, and she said—or rather, she thought—I mean, she decided—"

"Pull yourself together, boy," the headmaster said sternly. "Miss Thorpe *said*, Miss Thorpe *thought*, Miss Thorpe *decided*! This is getting us nowhere. Where is Miss Thorpe, anyway?"

Jennings looked at the ground and shuffled his feet. "We've lost her, sir."

"*Lost* her!"

"Only for the time being, of course. The warden
wouldn't let her stay because of the double yellow
lines in the High Street."

Mr. Pemberton-Oakes fretted with impatience. He
knew all about the double yellow lines in the High
Street! Indeed, it was for this reason that he had left
his car in Denton Street, earlier in the afternoon, and
had been on his way back to it when the sounds of
music and the signs of activity in the roadway had
attracted his attention.

"Now, listen to me, Jennings! I don't know what's
been happening, but I intend to find out. Miss Thorpe
appears to be the link in this mysterious chain of
circumstances and as soon as I can discover her where-
abouts——"

But at that moment the missing link, in person, came
pattering along the street, her face lighting up in
recognition as she caught sight of Jennings and Darbishire.

"So there you are! At last! I'm so glad I've found
you." Then she noticed the headmaster and acknowl-
edged him with a friendly nod. "Dear me, the trouble
I've had! The man in the music shop was most un-
helpful—and very rude, too—and I was in despair
until somebody outside the supermarket told me they'd
seen the piano being wheeled along here. But all's well
that ends well!" She peered through the crowd at the
cavorting dancers and waved a hand gaily in time with
the music. "And an open-air concert in full swing, too.
How perfectly splendid!"

Mr. Pemberton-Oakes stifled his exasperation. Politely, but firmly, he said: "Miss Thorpe, there appears
to be some misunderstanding. I was led to believe that

you wanted these boys to help you take—ah—apples and things around the village in my trailer."

"Apples?" She cocked her head sideways like a sparrow sighting a centipede. "No, no, not apples—pianos. Well, *one* piano, anyway. I thought I had made it quite clear when I telephoned. It must have been that woman who took the message. I thought she didn't sound very quick on the uptake."

Briefly, she explained the purpose of the afternoon's project, taking the responsibility upon herself and commending the boys in glowing terms for their eagerness to help the good work forward.

"You must be very proud of them, Mr. Oakes," she finished up. "I'm sure you'd have only been too willing for them to have come along, if you'd known what we'd been planning to do."

The headmaster forced a wan smile. Knowing Jennings and his companions, he suspected that there was more in this than met the eye, but he decided not to probe the matter too deeply.

"Naturally, I am pleased with their initiative, but I cannot wholly approve of their taking part in a street performance of this kind," he said. "I had no idea that anything like this was contemplated."

"Oh, but it wasn't, sir. It wasn't in the plan at all—it just happened," Jennings explained. He felt more at ease now that Miss Thorpe had rallied so staunchly to their support. "It was just that the music shop wouldn't take it, so we gave it to the Youth Club instead."

By now the rousing finale had come to an end, the crowd was dispersing, and the sturdier members of the Youth Club were manhandling the piano into their premises to continue the rehearsal indoors.

Andy Chester approached. "Where's that lad with

the collecting-tin?" he sang out, making a bee-line for Jennings. "We owe you something for the old honky-tonk."

Jennings felt embarrassed with the headmaster standing by, listening. "Oh, that's all right, Mr. Chester. We had to get rid of it, in any case. We don't expect you to pay for it."

"We'll make a contribution, anyway. When the cast heard you'd been hoping to flog it for charity they reckoned we ought to do something about it." Andy Chester took two pound notes from his pocket and dropped them in the tin. "With the compliments and thanks of the Dunhambury Youth Club," he said, grinning. "We're not a wealthy bunch of folks around here, but we know we're a jolly sight better off than the people you're collecting for!"

Mr. Pemberton-Oakes drove the boys back to school in his car. Miss Thorpe was so exhausted by the events of the afternoon that she decided to call at Ye Olde Tudor Bunne Shoppe for a cup of tea to recover her strength for the return journey.

"I'll bring the trailer back this evening, Mr. Oakes," she said as they took leave of her by the headmaster's car in Denton Street.

"Or we could go down to the cottage and fetch it tomorrow, couldn't we, sir!" Jennings volunteered.

The headmaster winced and drew a sharp breath. "No, Jennings, that's one thing you *won't* be doing," he said firmly. "Although I am prepared to overlook certain aspects of your conduct this afternoon, I have decided that, for the sake of the smooth running of the school routine, neither you nor any of your present companions will be allowed to set foot outside the premises for the rest of the term."

"Yes, sir! Sorry, sir."

"And now," the headmaster went on, throwing open the door of the car. "Get in quickly all of you, before I change my mind and give you the punishment you deserve for trying to pull the wool over my eyes!"

Jennings sat up in bed in Dormitory 4 that evening working out sums on the back of an envelope.

"We got twenty-three pence for the guy outside Linbury Stores that time, and four pounds, ninety-two pence at the bonfire collection," he announced to the members of the ginger-group as they waited for Mr. Carter to come in to put out the light. "So if you add on the two pounds, seventy-five pence we collected this afternoon, plus another two pounds for the piano, that makes a grand total of nine pounds, ninety pence that we've handed over to Mr. Carter for his worthy cause."

"Not bad," said Atkinson. "Pity we couldn't make it a round figure—ten pounds exactly."

"We could, if we each forked out a bit," Temple suggested. "It'd only come to two pence each for the five of us."

Jennings shook his head. "No, this project has got to be only what we *earn*. Anybody can *give* money if they're lucky enough to have it, but earning is different. You've got to use your brains and do a lot of hard work as well."

Mr. Carter noticed Jennings' thoughtful expression when he came in to call silence a few minutes later. "You look serious, Jennings," he said. "Anything the matter?"

The boy shook his head. "Just brooding, sir," he replied. "I was stirring up the old think-tank to see how I could earn another ten pence for your famine relief project, that's all."

Mr. Carter smiled. "Very kind of you, Jennings." He turned out the light. "I expect you'll think of a way. Trust you!"

Mr. Carter sat at the master's desk in Classroom 3 with a pile of work-books before him. It was the last lesson on Friday afternoon, and this week, in particular, the period was producing good results.

More than a fortnight had elapsed since Bonfire Night, yet the theme of the fireworks celebrations still dominated the written work of the form.

Bromwich and Martin-Jones, working together, had written a technical article on *The Preparation of Rocket Launching Sites* which contained useful advice about standing well back from the touch-paper when igniting low-priced missiles liable to fly off on an unpredictable course.

Venables' description of the barbecue supper, Temple's poem about torchlight processions, and Atkinson's essay on *The Duties of a Public Relations Officer to a Deceased Person* all made good reading; though not, perhaps, in the same class as Darbishire's scholarly research into *The Political Results of the Gunpowder Plot*, 1605.

Jennings, too, had produced some good work. He had forsaken his favourite topic of expeditions into Space and encounters with little green men. Instead, he had contributed a thoughtful piece of writing about the need for raising funds to help the poorer countries of the world to improve the living-standards of their peoples.

Mr. Carter was impressed. "This is quite the best

thing you've ever done, Jennings," he said, looking up from the book with a smile of encouragement. "In fact, I should like—with your permission—to include extracts from it in the next number of the school magazine."

Jennings was delighted. "I took ever such a lot of trouble with it, sir. I was hoping you'd agree to put a chunk in the mag. I had special reasons, you see, sir."

"Indeed! What reasons, may I ask?"

Jennings left his place in the back row and came and stood beside Mr. Carter at the master's desk. With an ink-smudged forefinger he pointed to the warning inscribed below the title of his essay: © *Copyright by J. C. T. Jennings. This piece of writing is copyright and may not be reproduced without written permission of the author. Film, television and radio telescope rights reserved.*

"I'll give you my written permission to print it, sir, but only on one condition: you have to pay a special fee of ten pence."

Mr. Carter raised a surprised eyebrow. He wasn't used to demands of this sort.

"Oh, it's not for *me*, sir. I don't want the money for myself," the author assured him. "It's just that we haven't quite reached our ten-pound target for the famine relief fund." He paused and smiled modestly. "So I thought I'd try and earn the last little bit by doing a piece of work that was worth—say—about ten pence."

Mr. Carter thought for a while before replying. He certainly wasn't going to make a practice of encouraging this sort of literary blackmail! . . . On the other hand, this was a special case. He, himself, had started the ball rolling: it would be a pity to stand in its way now that it had reached the goal-mouth.

"All right, Jennings," he said, and fumbled in his pocket for a ten pence piece.

"Thank you, sir .... Thank you very much, sir." And with a frown of importance the boy added: "It'll be quite safe with me, sir, for the time being. We shall be paying it into your special relief fund as soon as our treasurer has balanced his accounts."

Form 3 expressed their delight with a buzz of excitement as Jennings made his way back to his desk and dropped the coin into his coffee tin.

"Good old Jennings! Good old ginger-group! Good old Form 3 Fireworks Fund!" said Venables.

Darbishire put his hand up and said: "Sir, please, sir! It took an awful lot of thinking out—that plan to raise the last ten pence. I thought it might not come off, but Jennings managed it all right, didn't he, sir!"

Mr. Carter nodded. "Trust Jennings!" he said.